The Hollywood Takes

By Michael de Larrabeiti

THE HOLLYWOOD TAKES
THE PROVENÇAL TALES
THE BORRIBLES: ACROSS THE DARK METROPOLIS
IGAMOR
THE BORRIBLES GO FOR BROKE
THE BUNCE
A ROSE BEYOND THE THAMES
THE BORRIBLES
REDWATER RAID

The Hollywood Takes

MICHAEL DE LARRABEITI

A Crime Club Book
Doubleday
NEW YORK   LONDON   TORONTO   SYDNEY

A Crime Club Book

Published by Doubleday, a division of
Bantam Doubleday Dell Publishing Group, Inc.
666 Fifth Avenue, New York, New York 10103

Crime Club, Doubleday and the portrayal of a man with
a gun are trademarks of Doubleday, a division of
Bantam Doubleday Dell Publishing Group, Inc.

Library of Congress Cataloging-in-Publication Data
De Larrabeiti, Michael.
The Hollywood takes.
I. Title.
PR6054.E134H65   1988   823'.914   87-36522
ISBN 0-385-24622-6
Copyright © 1988 by Michael de Larrabeiti
All Rights Reserved
Printed in the United States of America
First Edition

OG

For Bernard Mattimore

"It's not the time it takes to take the takes that takes the time it takes, it's the time between the takes that takes the time it takes to take the takes—that's what it takes."

The Hollywood Takes

1

The Way to the Stars

"All I know is that he's dead," said Ernie, "and I need someone to take his place, right away."

I walked with the phone so that I could look out the window at the rain in the street.

"How did he get killed?" I asked.

"I don't know exactly. They only just told me about it. I think a ten-ton truck drove over his liver." Ernie's humour was hard, always had been. I could imagine his face, heavy round the receiver, square and belligerent, a face that I had often seen creased with an expression of triumphant dissatisfaction. Ernie is a free-lance cameraman in film and video. When he needs an assistant he often asks me, not because I'm particularly good as an assistant, I'm not, but because Ernie can be difficult to get on with at times and I know his ways. I'm a good listener, I nod a lot when people talk. My wife is convinced that if Ernie knew how spineless I really was he'd never employ me.

"It's two weeks in Los Angeles," Ernie went on, "some scenes for a commercial, Matrix Films, something to do with an after-shave called 'Espionage.' Deegan, that actor from the tele-series. We leave in two days."

"David Deegan," I said. "Yeah I know, 'Espionage.' Terrific. I've never been to the States."

"The producer's a chap called Tony, Tony Maretta . . . the director's Alex Boase. Can you do it?"

"Two weeks on location," I said.

My wife came into the room with the second child on her hip. The first one was at school. She leant against the door jamb and smiled, like Torquemada. There are certain key words she hates: location, re-shoot, clappers-loader, stuff like that. She thinks I bask in reflected film business glory. I do a bit, but then it's not my fault. I've never done anything else except make films.

I flicked over the pages of my work diary. They were blank. "What's the money?"

Ernie laughed. "Better than you normally earn, believe you me. Well?"

"Yeah, I can do it," I said.

"Good. Then you'd better get up to Matrix offices right away and check through the equipment. It's thirty-five mill. The real stuff. Make sure everything's there. Then you'll have to do the carnet for customs. Rapps might have done it already."

"Rapps?"

"The one who got killed. Ring me when it's all finished and I'll get Matrix to ship it all to Heathrow. Oh, while you're out get me a dozen golf balls. The hotel we're staying at has a golf course."

Ernie put the phone down then and so did I. "California," I said, in the direction of the doorway, "two weeks."

"That's good, we need the money." My wife swapped the child from one hip to the other. I tried one of my sycophantic smiles on her but she just stared at me like I was a strange and useless souvenir purchased in some unknown country and left on the mantelpiece by someone she didn't like. It was a look that isolated me and left me all alone. We didn't like each other very much any more. There were days when it was hard to know why we bothered staying together—the kids maybe.

Outside I slammed the street door behind me and took a deep breath of freedom. It should have been July but wasn't. The rain was squalling, slinging itself against my face like handfuls of grit, an insult in summer. Above me a plane roared and levelled off for Heathrow. I looked for it but it remained invisible behind low clouds and all I got was rain in my eye.

I buttoned my coat, bent my head against the weather and went out of the cul-de-sac where I lived. In about ten years' time it would be a better place; now it was just drab, too many of its terraced houses un-painted, mine amongst them. I had one of the cheaper ones near the railway embankment. Mortlake was away to my right and Putney to my left. From the way it sounds it should have been better than it was, but everything could have been better. My house could have been paid for and the sun could have been shining and my wife could have been a pleasure to live with.

At the end of the street the cars were bumper to bumper, waiting for the level crossing to open, their windscreen wipers flouncing. As I walked to the bus stop a train went by on its way to Clapham Junction and Waterloo. The cars revved their engines and slipped into gear. High above, another jumbo lowered itself towards the airport. Up there was all right. Up there it wasn't raining and the sky was golden blue. Up there were real people sitting in rows, sipping iced whisky, coming back from real places. I blinked my eyes in the wet. There was nothing real about down here, nothing at all. Just because I lived here didn't make it real. Quite the opposite. The things I hoped for were elsewhere—somewhere over the rainbow— that place that was away from black and white and existed only in Technicolor.

I reached the bus stop and grinned at the half a dozen individuals standing there. Well, it was my turn now. Never mind that woman I lived with. Never mind my scant hair and the sapless skin, and never mind the fact that I was forty and too old to be a camera-assistant. Yes, it was my turn now. I was the one going off into the golden yonder.

When I got to the Matrix offices there was only a secretary to be seen, attacking her nails with a file as long as a sabre.

"They're all away," she said.

I watched the water run down my raincoat and make pools on the oatmeal carpet. Around me the desk and chairs were chrome and the walls were silver flecked. "I know," I said, "I've come to check the gear and do a carnet."

"Oh," said the secretary, "you must be Del. Someone phoned me about you. You'll find the gear in the camera room, downstairs at the end of the corridor. Wasn't it terrible about Phil Rapps?"

"Who?"

"The assistant who got killed."

"It certainly was for him," I said, "but it wasn't for me. I need the work."

It took me about two hours to do what I had to do. I ran the camera, made sure the tripods moved easily and inspected the magazines and lenses. Most tiresome of all was the writing out of the carnet but at last even that was done and I could mark each of the fifteen silver boxes with labels that said, "Atlantic-Pacific-Airways, Los Angeles."

As I finished the last one the door opened and the secretary came in bearing a mug of coffee.

"Thanks," I said. "Do you know anything about this?"

I pointed to the ditty-bag that, I imagined, had belonged to the dead assistant, Rapps. It was a round canvas bag, with pockets in the sides, like anglers use. It had a sturdy strap so that it could be slung from the shoulder, and a circular wooden bottom about an inch thick. I had one almost the same at home and it went on every job I did. I had inspected this one earlier and it contained all the things that assistants carry with them: camera tape, screwdrivers, torches, a can of compressed air and some Blutack.

There was also a beautifully constructed wooden clapper-board about twelve inches by nine which Rapps must have made for himself in his spare time. I already had a large clapper-board in the accessories case but something small was always useful for close-ups.

"Oh that belonged to Rapps," said the secretary. "I don't know what to do with it . . . he wasn't married. I suppose you might as well have it."

So I took it and was pleased I did. It was a lot better than mine—it looked more professional for a start, and there was something extra in it that made me smile. My predecessor must have done Ernie's shopping for him. In one of the bag's side-pockets was a box of a dozen top-quality golf balls. Ernie would be very pleased with me. It certainly was an ill wind that blew no one any good at all.

I met Ernie at seven o'clock in the evening two days later. I found him by the Atlantic-Pacific-Airways desk sur-

rounded by the gear. "It's just arrived," he said. "I'm waiting for Nick Fitch. He's got the sound gear and the tickets."

Nick was the recordist. The rest of the crew were already in Los Angeles and had been for some five or six
days. I had never worked with Nick but there was no
mistaking him as he advanced through the crowd. He was
followed by a trolley-load of silver boxes pushed along by a
baggage handler in green overalls.

Nick was a handsome man of just over thirty with a
good profile and receding hair which made him look more
mature than he was. He was dressed with great care in
casual clothes. A well-cut sports jacket of the palest blue,
designer jeans, white mutton-cloth shirt with a pale brown
stripe and cream-coloured leather shoes. His bearing, an
erect and wary stroll, a slightly upward gaze, made me
think of a ruthless CIA killer cast for an international
movie. In fact Nick was modest, shy and sincere. A great
romantic, a man who needed women.

"We'd best get this gear to the shipping agent," he said.
"They'll do the rest."

"How many pieces all together?" asked the porter,
"that's including personal cases but not cabin baggage?"

"With my ditty-bag it'll make twenty-six," I said, and I
gave him a tenner.

The plane was a 747 and it was carrying about three hundred and fifty passengers. I sat in a gangway seat because
flying makes me very frightened and I do not like to see
out the window.

"Are you scared?" asked Nick.

I nodded. "Scared of everything," I answered, "but especially scared of flying."

Ernie clipped the buckle of his seat-belt and adjusted it so that it fitted snugly against his solid stomach. "I had to film an air-crash once, for the news . . ." He let the sentence hang in the air like a raven looking for somewhere to roost.

"What's Los Angeles like?" I asked.

Ernie laughed. "It's so crazy that even the rest of America thinks it's crazy."

The plane was full and the seats too close together. There were lots of children and they cried in relays. I slept and I read. Every now and then the cabin staff came at us with food and drink, their eyes glazed. Eleven hours after leaving Heathrow we landed at Los Angeles International at about one o'clock in the morning, local time, and all our luggage, both camera equipment and personal, was impounded by the customs.

"I knew it," said Ernie. "I knew it."

"But we need the gear," said Ronnie. "We're meant to be filming tomorrow."

The customs man stuck more red labels on the silver boxes. "I can't help you," he said. "There's a lot of equipment here and in Hollywood it could sell overnight. Unless your company posts a bond of fifteen thousand dollars we can't let it into the country."

"What about the personal stuff, you don't need that?"

"I'm sorry but we have to check through that too, just to be sure."

Ronnie twitched. He was the unit manager, about twenty-five, slight and skinny with a foxy face and a too-ready smile.

"My ditty-bag's gone missing," I said. "You'd better tell

Atlantic-Pacific. It's an olive green canvas bag, like fisher-
men use."

Ronnie nodded and twitched again. He wrote something
on his pad. "That's all I need," he said. "It'll be halfway to
Tahiti by now."

Outside in the dark, Ronnie had a micro-bus waiting. "I
thought we'd need it for the gear," he said.

He drove as nervously as he did everything else and the
bus tipped from side to side at every bend. I gripped the
edge of my window and peered out. I felt proud of myself.

Here I was on the San Diego Freeway, six lanes in both
directions, a haze of flashing lights, yellow and white and
red, a never-ending circus of cars, swooping and surging
and passing on both sides. And hundreds of advertise-
ments too, above and below us as the highway rose and
fell. Colours clashed and broke in my sight and the smell
of exhaust fumes and factory chimneys filled my nostrils.

But best of all was the sight of the illuminated sign-posts
speeding by me, almost too quickly to be read: Monterey,
Pasadena, Long Beach, Studio City, Metro-Goldwyn-
Mayer, Santa Monica, Paramount, Beverly Hills, Culver
City, San Fernando Valley, Sunset Boulevard.

"Jesus," I said. "All these places, all these names. Just
think . . . I'm in Hollywood."

2

The Wizard of Oz

"Sunny-side up?" asked the waitress, leaning forward and flexing her breasts like a weight-lifter testing his biceps. She had blonde hair the colour of pink candy and a loose mouth with purple lipstick on it. She licked her pencil and hooked one buttock up so that it was higher than the other.

"Marvellous," said Ernie, "more'n fifty years making films out here and they all still think they're acting in one."

"I'll have hash browns and bacon and sausages and tomatoes and two eggs and some toast."

"Yuwanzumgwaffee?" she said, writing and smiling at the same time into the space above my head. She was wearing a mini-skirt with a tiny white apron pinned onto it. Her movements were abrupt and her eyes, switching from left to right, watched the other tables where one or two couples and a group of seven or eight men were finishing lunch. It was three in the afternoon and we had just got up.

"Same for me," said Ernie.

"And me," said Nick, unable to lift his gaze from the waitress's breasts.

She ignored him and turned her head to look towards the kitchen. "You stayin' hyah?"

We showed our room keys and the waitress yawned and snatched our menus from us like a school-mistress confiscating pornographic literature, then she marched away on big firm legs like a soldier.

The three of us were sitting in the restaurant of the Treetops Hotel somewhere to the north of Los Angeles proper. It was spacious and dark and cool. Outside, beyond an enormous window of plate glass, the sun blazed down on a parkland made shady with pine, sycamore and eucalyptus. The brocaded lawns were watered by remote control and the flower-beds were tended by tongueless Mexicans, their brows permanently creased with secret thoughts. Watching them work were the chipmunks and squirrels that ran freely everywhere. At the entrance to our restaurant was a small car-park for new arrivals and along one edge of it ran the other wing of the building in which we sat, containing the reception and executive offices.

The accommodation itself was located in about twenty brick-built, shingle-roofed pavilions, each one situated at some distance from the next, and all of them half hidden amongst the trees and bushes. Each pavilion had twelve rooms, six on the ground floor and six above. The upper rooms had a private balcony, the lower ones a terrace with a sliding window that gave access to it.

I had a room on the ground floor of pavilion seven. It was wide and clean and furnished with mock antiques from an uncertain century. It was also provided with freshly wrapped soap, tumblers sealed in cling foil and a lavatory seat that was sterilised every morning.

Not only that but there were two swimming pools, tennis courts and a comfortable club-house for the hundreds of golfers who visited Treetops to try out the pleasures of its eighteen-hole course. I had been dropped into a truly luxurious setting, a place that top Hollywood people frequented day in and day out, and I took to it right away.

In a little while a Mexican waiter arrived with our breakfasts and poured us some coffee. As we ate I noticed that the group on the far side of the room were studying us with unusual attention. Then the man at the head of their table pushed back his chair and walked, loose-jointed and relaxed, across the restaurant.

He approached us as if he'd been aimed at such a destiny from the moment God had touched Adam's finger, and his smile was firm and architectural as he advanced. It was as if there was nothing he couldn't do; as if his every word would become law the moment he uttered it. He was handsome and tall, and once you'd looked at him, it was difficult to look at anything or anyone else.

He came right up to our table and leant over it, his big hands on the cloth, his arms rigid. His hair was thick and all of a piece, black going silver. His eyes were bright grey stones and never flinched.

"I had to come over and introduce myself," he said; his voice was warm and, at that moment, benign, like a moist tumour. "I am the Reverend J. Turrill." He looked at us all in turn as if he expected one of us to say something. Nobody did. I stared at the Reverend's suit. It was pale blue and had been hand-made from expensive material. His wrist watch was gold and worth more than I could earn in two years, maybe three. His finger-nails were clean and polished.

At last Ernie nodded and lifted his coffee cup. Ernie doesn't like leaving London but once he has he will talk to anybody, unafraid of conversation with the strangest of strangers.

The Reverend put a visiting card on the table as if he were laying the ace in a royal flush; as if it should have meant something important to us all. It was a fawn-coloured one with the print in dark brown. I leant forward and read:

THE REVEREND J. TURRILL
At the Church of God's Will
Be ye reconciled to God and his ineffable purpose
All ye who are lonely and sick of heart,
come unto us

"Are you selling *Watchtower* or something?" asked Ernie.

The Reverend lowered his body into a chair and purred at us with his voice. "I sell you nothing," he said. "On the contrary I have the greatest gift on God's earth, and I am giving it away—the knowledge of the Lord. Where are you from?"

"Potter's Bar," said Ernie.

"That means London," said Nick.

"Wonderful," answered the Reverend. Now he turned to me as though I might have some special thing to say. "And what are you doing here?"

"We're shooting some scenes for a series of commercials, for British television."

"I thought so," said the Reverend. "It's films or real-estate or cars out here. You look like film people." He scrutinised me again. "What do you do?"

"Camera-assistant," I said, pouring myself another cup of coffee.

"He's only here because someone got killed," said Ernie. "Probably did it himself to get the work."

"Oh really," said the Reverend. His perusal of me intensified and I didn't like it. It was as if the wrong person were still alive. "Then there must be a message."

"Message?"

"You mean from the other side?" Ernie laughed, pleased that Los Angeles was living up to its reputation for bizarre inhabitants. He filled a clean cup with coffee and placed it in front of our guest. "It's no good trying to convert us, we'll be going home in two weeks' time."

The Reverend raised his cup and sipped, his big stone eyes steady on my face. "I know all about you," he said, "and I know why you are here. You will need protection. This is where the yellow brick road ends. It is a dangerous place."

I nodded wisely and wished the man would go away. He was spooky. I shuddered and glanced at Ernie and Nick but they only smiled, enjoying themselves.

"I need your message," said the Reverend. "I bear a heavy responsibility to my Church and the people in it. There are hundreds of thousands here, lonely, damned. It is my duty to find those whom the Lord has written in the book of the redeemed."

"I wish the Lord would get our gear out of customs," said Nick.

"Your equipment will be returned to you this evening."

"Well if that happens," said Ernie, "I'll join your Church myself."

"It is not you I want. I know all the faces."

"Faces?"

"Yes, the faces of the people I have saved and those I am going to save."

With an effort I moved my head and looked through the restaurant window, beyond the terrace and into the park-land of lawn and trees.

"Any of those faces here?" asked Nick.

The Reverend looked at him. "Saved, no," he said. There was passion in the voice now and Nick paled a little under the force of it.

"Damned?"

"Oh yes," said the Reverend, and he rolled his eyes round in a slow arc, like fully loaded cannon, until they were aimed at me. "His," he said, and Ernie hooted in merriment. "Unless he does what God has given him to do then he will die."

My stomach shrivelled and the sunshine outside wavered and went cold. Someone was dancing on my grave.

Nick blushed. "Ker-rist," he said.

The Reverend rose from his seat, rising in one surge like the end of the world, his countenance shining like a halle-lujah. "I have brought you the word," he said. "You had better heed it."

With this he turned away his beatific face, and his six or seven followers, all of them as massive as their leader, left their table and greeted him with loving smiles. Then the group walked from the restaurant, and beyond the terrace an enormous stretch limousine, black and twice the length of any ordinary automobile, swung to a halt by the steps at reception.

We watched and waited and in a moment the Reverend and his men came down the steps, disappeared behind the sightless windows of their car and were driven away.

"Jesus," said Nick, "some church that can afford limos like that one."

"See what I said," cried Ernie, triumphant, as if he'd

just invented California himself, "this place is full of loonies, full of 'em."

I said nothing. The Reverend had frightened me to death. For the first time in my life I felt as if I'd been doomed.

3

A Shot in the Dark

Tony Maretta, the producer, found Ernie and me in the bar that evening. He came across and lounged near us with all the assurance of an immortal.

"Ronnie's just got back with the gear," he said. "It's all there but it's been thoroughly searched, personal luggage as well. Funny that. Have a drink?"

"White wine," I said, "medium."

Maretta was young, about twenty-eight or -nine, five feet ten with legs that were too short for his long torso. His thick black hair sprouted in tight curls over his skull like a bonnet. He had pale eyes and his face was round with contours that shifted visibly with his moods, its edges never firm. I took a dislike to him immediately.

The drinks arrived and he smiled. The week or so that Tony had already spent on location had varnished him with a one-piece Californian tan and an easy American affability. He shot his white shirt cuffs out of the sleeves of his fawn light-weight suit and looked at me, softening his expression with the careless pity that the young and handsome lavish on the old and ugly.

"We'll be shooting on Newport Beach tomorrow," he said. "I've rented a couple of big houses for a few days."

I finished my drink. "I'd better go and look at the gear,"
I said, "and hang my clothes up."

Ernie stood up to his knees in the Pacific Ocean and held
the camera on his shoulder, out of reach of the waves that
rose, every now and then, to his thighs. I stood beside him
and Nick stood behind us on the sand. We were all dressed
in bathing trunks and baseball caps. Ernie was finishing a
joke.

". . . and the countess said, 'Don't scream when you
reach my balls, I'm really the Scarlet Pimpernel in dis-
guise.' "

A wave flopped and swamped us to the waist. I gazed
out across the water to where Deegan was pushing his surf
board away from us. It was the end of the day and he'd
had enough. We'd been filming since early morning and
Deegan had no gift for water sports.

I moved out of the water and got my legs into the sun.
The Pacific was cold and my feet were beyond feeling. Ten
yards further up the beach lay a woman on a sun-bed—an
actress called Millie, shipped in from an agency for the
final shots of the day: the après-ski, the glamorous life-
style, the candle-lit dinner on the verandah of the Malibu
house, all brought about by Espionage, the magical after-
shave.

I pushed Espionage over a precipice in my mind and
forgot it and contemplated Millie's body instead. She lay
to attention, staring at the sky from behind big, dinner-
plate sun-glasses, her plump breasts flattened under their
own weight, stranded like jelly fish.

In the distance Deegan clambered onto his surf board.
Alex came alive and said, "Turn over," and I went back

into the water and stood by Ernie. This time Deegan did not fall off and the shot worked.

"I got plenty there," said Ernie. "You can wrap."

"Thank Christ," said Alex, and plunged into the water as if bent on suicide.

Deegan arrived on the beach. He looked tired. "I've had enough of the Pacific Ocean," he said, and sat himself in a white canvas chair under a multi-coloured parasol. The rainbow that fell across his body and the shimmering reflections of the sunlit waves made him look like a tropical plant.

Millie raised her head and shaded her eyes. She smiled at Deegan, a full day's pay, and then lowered her head to her pillow. I watched Deegan collect the smile as his right and then pick up a copy of the Los Angeles *Times*.

Deegan was famous now but he'd not had an easy time. He had worked in a steel factory for ten years after leaving school, singing in pubs at weekends with a small rock group of his own. He'd been spotted eventually by the man who was to become his manager, Barry Keeling, and after only a few television appearances he'd been chosen to play the lead in a brand new series about the British Secret Service, with a night-club singer as its hero, and called, of course, "Espionage."

That had been three or four years ago and Deegan had made an immediate hit. He'd written the "Espionage" theme and the other spin-offs were enormous. Now there were the after-shave and deodorants. I looked at our star with a deep-seated envy. Only thirty and he was already a millionaire.

Ernie gave me the camera. "Put this away," he said. "We won't be shooting out here any more, the light's gone."

Tony cupped his hands to his mouth and shouted up to one of the houses, where Ronnie was lazing on the verandah. "Drinks," he yelled, and Ronnie disappeared through the sliding glass panels.

A Frisbee swooped and stalled overhead like a home-going swallow. As far as I could see in either direction stretched a line of holiday houses, and every five hundred yards or so, out on the beach, was a life-saver's hut on stilts. From the highest point of each hut the life-savers, bronzed and burnished like souvenir ash-trays, watched the sea, watched in their turn by damp-lapped girls. After a while Ronnie came out of the house carrying a large cool-bag and we sat on the sand, drinking Coca-Cola as the sun went down.

Millie had changed into a dress that was slashed to her midriff and the evening sat on her just as easily as the day had done. Her hair was perfect and her lips were moist with scarlet lipstick. Deegan had changed too and was dressed as for the part he played in his series—white tuxedo, red bow-tie.

The shots on the porch went well, dusk surrounding the candlelight. Millie leant towards Deegan, put her body into her eyes and handed it over.

"Ah," said Ernie, from the bottom of a deep silence, "if only insignificance were as powerful an aphrodisiac as fame we might all, tonight, be lying between golden thighs."

Later, upstairs in the large sitting room with its window open onto the verandah, we sat at a long table and a girl called Angela brought in a meal from the nearest Chinese restaurant.

"She's just some girl Ronnie hired," said Nick, "to take stills and be a runner."

Angela was as tall and as big-bosomed as Millie but she went in for the natural look. Her blonde hair had been bleached almost white by the sun and she wore no make-up. She didn't need to. She was simply dressed in jeans, a shirt, and sneakers. She was the type of woman who never even noticed men like me. If I stood on tip-toe I might get to kiss her on the knee.

Nick fell in love with her the moment he saw her but she didn't notice him either. There was something else, or someone else, on her mind most of the time and it showed in the way she screwed her face up and bit her lips.

After the meal she took the plates away and Ronnie opened some bottles of Californian champagne. Millie laid her head in Deegan's lap where he sat on the long sofa, and he sang to her in a whisper.

I went out onto the verandah with Nick, both of us with full glasses. Out in the dark I stared into the sky; the stars were near enough to touch. Below me the waves were breaking on the shore and for a moment it was too perfect, too unreal, like being part of a feature film in which I was both actor and audience.

"Too good to be true this is," I said, "isn't it?"

"Oh no it isn't." Angela had come to stand behind me. "This is real all right. I come from a place called Waterlooville. That's Iowa. Iowa is a field of corn a thousand miles long. It's so hot there in summer you can hear the ground crack. This is real. I tell you, this is real."

Angela pronounced these words with such ferocity that I stepped back into the room. It was then that the four Mexicans appeared. At least they looked like Mexicans to me, only they were bigger than the waiters at the hotel, and they were quiet and efficient too. I think I was the first one of us to notice them and I wondered what they were doing in our place, especially as they all carried guns. Had the house been double-booked?

Gradually the room went quiet and there were some shouts downstairs. A door slammed. I swallowed hard. What kind of a country was this? Perhaps Ernie was right and the whole population thought they were making a major motion picture.

The biggest of the Mexicans moved towards Tony; the others covered the kitchen area and the stairs.

"Your luggage," said the big one to Tony, "and the equipment." He didn't need to ask who was in charge.

Tony tried to stand up but he was deep in an armchair and before he could get out of it the Mexican had pushed him backwards with a foot.

"Who the hell are you anyway?" said Tony. He was angry but not afraid.

"Baeza," said the Mexican.

"The equipment's all in the next room," I said. "The luggage is in the bedrooms, next door too."

Baeza said something in Spanish and one of his companions called downstairs and two more men appeared and went into the adjoining room.

"What the hell are you doing?" said Tony. He was not used to being bullied. His life hadn't been like mine.

"I am looking for something," said Baeza, "and if you try to stop me you will be hurt." Baeza seemed to have taken a dislike to Tony but then most people did.

"We haven't got anything belonging to you," said Alex, speaking quietly. He was sitting at the kitchen bar and a guard with a gun stood behind him.

"I didn't say it belonged to me," said Baeza. "I just want it and I think one of you might have it."

I shuddered and was glad I knew nothing.

"You've got the wrong house," said Tony. "We've only just arrived from England."

Baeza smiled. "I know where you are from," he said, "and I know what I want. One of you has already died because of it. We are not afraid to do it again."

From the next room there came the sound of a violent searching as our boxes were upended and the contents dumped out of them. After a while one of the Mexicans came through the door with some film cans and pulled the stock out of them. Ernie looked a question at me but I shook my head. I had already unloaded the day's footage and sent it to the laboratories by cab.

The moment the Mexicans had finished with the equipment they started on our luggage and when they still hadn't found what they wanted they started on us. Heavy fingers probed the recesses of our clothing and felt in our pockets. Most of us were still in shorts and shirts only, so the body searches did not take long; it took longer for the two women.

"Shit!" said Millie, when they'd finished with her. "It's always the same in this town. If it ain't agents or producers it's wetbacks. They all want to feel yer ass."

Then the Mexicans began to move from the room and at the head of the stairs Baeza, still with the gun in his hand, halted. "You'll be seeing me again," he said.

"Tell us what you want," said Alex, "for Christ's sake."

"One of you knows," Baeza replied, "and next time we will know who that person is. Then it will not be so easy for you." And with that he turned and ran down the stairs.

There was a silence amongst us as we listened to the cars

drive away, and it was into this silence that Deegan sent his voice, continuing the song he had been whispering to Millie earlier.

I had never heard him sing before, except in his series, and the sound was clear and strong. He sang a ballad about a young girl dressing for her wedding day, how beautiful she felt as she stood naked, how wonderful she felt dressed. It was a brave song, looking forward to the unknown years, daring them to come and do their worst. It was a song I could never have sung. Deegan wanted the years; I was afraid of them.

But the song dismissed our shame and our fear. When it was over we all applauded and Ronnie opened more champagne and filled our glasses. We drank a toast to ourselves and Millie's eyes shone and she kissed Deegan full on the lips. She was his for as long as he wanted her—just as certainly as the dark Pacific was beating on the shore only a yard or two beyond the window.

I slept badly. All night there had been a heavy wedge of dreams lying on my chest, and there had been no comfort in them. Early, very early for me, I left my bed, where the sheets were wound in grimy ropes, and crept from the house, picking my way across the fag-end rubbish of our evening's ash, stealing across the empty and edgeless beach.

I awoke then. The cool grey space rushed at me and made me shiver. The air was moist and still touched with darkness. I drew it into my lungs and warmed it. Far out in the unmoving metal of the sea a lonely head lay on the water, hardly disturbing it with a single ripple. A thin mist was hanging, mast high, like a spell along the horizon. I walked slowly, kicking my bare feet in the loose sand.

Halfway to the water-line I sank to my haunches. I felt immeasurably sad, the solitary swimmer in his contentment only adding to my melancholy.

The circle of earth and water that I could see was empty; not a ship, not a car. The sky was as solid as lead and the same colour. I could feel the push of three thousand miles at my back and beyond that another three thousand.

The swimmer hadn't moved. I shivered again and pulled on the sweater I had carried with me. I had thought of a swim, lying in bed, but I had been warm there. Out here in the cold I lacked the courage of the man in the water and I remained on land.

This cowardice in me plucked at a chord of self-pity. The film business was bad for me; unhealthy, my wife said. It obliged me to meet people with talent and money. The David Deegans and Tony Marettas had been to the moon and back but I would never even manage escape velocity. It would have been better for me to have driven a bread van through life, selling sliced loaves and coupling from time to time with greasy-skinned women, fumbling under their stiff aprons of flowered plastic, kissing their dog-biscuit faces.

The Deegans and the Marettas had all the things I pretended to scorn. They had drunk a magic potion concocted from advantage, experience, luck and money, and that potion gave, to those who drank it, the lustre of a Greek God. And the main ingredient of the recipe was the last— money. Only give me a hundred thousand pounds a year and I, too, could have balls of iron, a cock of fire and spermatozoa of molten gold.

Out of the motionless furrow of the grey sea an arm rose, then another, and a face turned and an arrow-head of ripple came towards me. As the swimmer approached I saw that it was Deegan. He walked from the water, dripping dark against the mist. He picked up his towel and smiled. He looked new, reborn, bright drops shining in his hair, his flesh content from its pleasures. He sat down beside me and smiled again, teeth perfect.

"Sparks flew from my anus last night, Del," he said. "It was like tobogganing down an electric bannister. Millie is a gem—the pursuit of happiness and professionalism all combined in her to make the American Dream come true."

"Yes," I said, "and what about those Mexicans, they scared the shit out of me."

"I don't know," answered Deegan. He lowered his head and rubbed his hair. The mist sailed away into the sky like a liberated balloon. The sea shrugged itself at the edges and threw down one or two waves. "Millie thought they'd mistook us for someone else. Some guys who had something for them, drugs maybe."

There was a shout from the house. We turned to see Ronnie on the verandah, waving. "Breakfast!" he yelled. "The yacht will be here soon."

"Those shots on the boat, is it?" Deegan stood and draped the towel around his shoulders. We looked north towards Long Beach, where a brown cloud was forming above the petro-chemical complex.

"We've still got the sunset shot to do," I said, "but they have good sunsets here, wonderful colours."

"Yes," said Deegan, "it's the pollution that does it." He started to walk away and I followed him, going towards the house, where the others, most of them, stood on the verandah watching.

4

To Catch a Thief

We left Newport Beach late in the afternoon two days later
and drove north to the Treetops Hotel, stopping for dinner
on the way. After the meal Ernie and I took the station-
wagon and went on. The others, looking for a night out,
went to a disco that Millie knew.

It was nearly midnight when Ernie and I got out of the
car in the silent parkland of Treetops and we talked for a
little while, hesitating before going to our rooms.

"Aw, we're not working in the morning," said Ernie at
last. "Let's have one for the road."

Agreeing without answering I followed him towards the
reception area, where there was a drinks machine and ice.
We shoved coins into a slot and each with a can of beer we
walked away from the lights to where some garden furniture stood amongst the trees and bushes.

Again the night sky was borne down by the weight of its
stars, but now there was a quality of menace in the darkness. As we looked back towards the lights outside reception, a car door opened and a woman appeared in silhou-
ette. She closed the door quietly and began to walk
towards us, her feet silent on the black grass, her shoes
dangling from her right hand.

She sat at our table without being asked and crossed her

legs. She was back-lit and it was difficult to see her face.
She seemed young, in her early twenties, with her straight
hair cut an inch or two above her shoulders. She was wearing what appeared to be a woollen dress. It lay close to her
body all over and came down to her knees. Her legs were
bare and her deodorant made her smell like a new box of
chocolates.

"Hello," said Ernie.

"Are you on vacation?" she asked.

"No."

"To play golf?"

"I wish I could, my friend lost the golf balls."

"We're filming," I said.

"Oh, anything I might know about?"

"We're doing some background shots for a commercial.
An after-shave called Espionage."

"Where are you from?"

"London."

"I've been to Europe," said the girl, as if the continent
were an isolation hospital. Her eyes gleamed in the darkness as she pulled on a cigarette.

"Did you like it?" asked Ernie.

"Yes," she said, then she fell silent. The night crept a
little closer. I could sense it thickening on the hills and
across the beaches. The girl leant back, thinking, but not
relaxed.

"Do you guys want some entertainment?" she said next,
speaking as if she'd just run up a steep hill.

"Are you going to take us to a party?"

Ernie was suspicious. "What do you mean?"

"Like this," said the girl, her voice calm now, and she
laid her cigarette carefully in the ashtray and undid the
front of her dress. Her breasts gleamed and shifted.

Ernie and I stared. The sudden shock of nakedness made the breasts exotic, the girl alien. I suppressed a snigger of nervousness and the slight sound tightened the silence, but the girl held her gaze steady, as if she were only a mere messenger, bringing gifts from a foreign land, her only function having been to open the casket.

When we had looked long enough she closed her dress, buttoned it, retrieved her cigarette and drew on it, as if nothing had happened.

Ernie finished his drink and jumped to his feet, angry. "I must go to bed," he said, and with that, before I had a chance to follow him, he had darted into the darkness.

The girl watched him go, turning her face towards the lights.

"How much is this entertainment?" I asked.

"A hundred and fifty dollars."

I considered the proposition. I was perhaps twenty years older than this girl, and even with my clothes still on, I felt slightly ridiculous in her presence. Then there was Ernie. I could imagine what he would say in the morning. While I was thinking the girl stood up.

"Come on," she said, "let's do it. Forget the money."

"Me? You don't even know what I look like."

"That's sometimes an advantage," said the girl, and she led the way across the grass towards the pavilion which held my bedroom, just as if I'd told her where it was.

I had never slept with an American woman before. In fact I haven't slept with very many women at all, and certainly with no woman that good-looking or that young. I was used only to grey and exhausted flesh. Did this kind of thing happen in Hollywood all the time?

It was like Deegan had said: professionalism applied to

the pursuit of happiness in bed. It was like nothing I had known—hard tense flesh at the service of a shameless and reckless energy. I couldn't believe it and didn't waste any time trying to.

The lamp by the side of the bed had remained on, and afterwards, in the light of it, she slipped away from me and crossed the room to the fridge. She filled two glasses with ice and poured scotch into them. Then she came back and handed me one of the drinks.

I could see now that her black hair was bobbed. She had an attractive, serious face and her skin was brown all over. Her breasts moved as she raised her glass to her mouth.

"I don't understand," I said. "You don't look right to be doing this."

She smiled very briefly. The sliding window onto the terrace was open and the smell of eucalyptus was in the room, mingling with the smell of the scotch and the smell of her.

"What's right?" she asked. "This is the quickest way I know of making money. Do you want me to dress up in a frilly skirt and put a white bow on my ass, like the waitresses here? I've tried these jobs. You spend so much time working for so little that you haven't got any energy left for any of the good things . . . and the guys who use the place all think you should go with them for nothing anyway. So . . . once or twice a week I do this . . . and I can live and do the things I wanna do. It isn't a drug, you know. I can stop when I like."

"Can you?"

"I can and do. Tell me a guy who would turn down the chance of sleeping with a different woman once or twice a week. I pick and choose. I charge a price for a service and you don't have to spend money taking me out to dinner, that's all."

"But why do it for free?"

The girl threw back her head and laughed. "There's no such thing as a free lunch," she said.

When I awoke in the morning she was in the bath, singing with the door open. I ordered breakfast for us both and when it arrived we took it on the terrace like two honeymooners. Already the sun was bright and the caddy-cars, white and battery powered, were humming their way to the links. Every now and then, from the distance, came the dry sound of a club striking a golf ball.

She poured some orange juice and studied my face. "You're in trouble," she said, and as she spoke I felt fear seize my heart. Something nasty was on the way: her jealous boyfriend was outside the door ready to blackmail me or beat me up; she had the disease.

I said nothing, too scared to think of anything. The skin on the back of my neck tensed.

"The Reverend came to see you . . ."

I spilled my orange juice. "The Reverend? You know the Reverend?"

She nodded. "He came to see you because you have something of his and he needs it. He said you'd understand the message."

"I don't understand the message, and I have no idea what's going on. Some damn Mexicans think we've got something of theirs too, but we haven't. He's got the wrong people."

She shrugged and spread some toast. "The Reverend doesn't get things wrong."

"Did he ask you to come here . . . I mean to see me?"

"Yes, he thinks you're trying to take his property for yourself. He can't let that happen."

I sprang to my feet, stepped into the sunshine and then back into the shade. "I'm scared," I said. "I really don't know what's going on."

She filled her coffee cup and mine too. "If you can convince the Reverend that you are speaking the truth then you'll be in the clear."

"And what if I can't?"

She took a sip from her cup and looked at me from under her eyebrows. "He's not a man you should cross," she said.

I took another turn around the room. "What can I do? What can I do?"

She stood and smoothed her dress over her hips and tossed her hair loose. "You said you weren't working until this afternoon?"

I shook my head.

"Then I'll take you to see the Reverend. I think that will impress him. It might even get you off the hook . . . it'll certainly give you a little more time, I guess."

"Go to see him! What'll he do?"

She laughed. "Nothing, at least not right away. You'll be all right."

"Did he send you to get me?" I asked.

The girl walked towards me and put her hands on my shoulders. Her eyes were grey I noticed and they looked at me with pity, as if I were incurably crippled. "Yes, he did."

I could see it all now. "Did he pay you too?"

Her gaze remained even, unwavering. "Yes," she said, "he did."

5

The Roots of Heaven

Barefoot she drove an apple green sports car with the hood down. Her hair blew across her face and her dress was drawn back so that it only covered the top inch or two of her legs.

"You look like Grace Kelly," I said.

That pleased her and she laughed. "Which movie?"

"I don't know . . . The one on the Riviera, I think."

I had no idea where we were going. The city was so long and so wide I never knew where I was. No matter where I went in those two weeks I always needed someone to guide me. What I do remember is that we eventually drove past a small and scruffy park where the ground showed through the grass like the grubby heel in a tramp's worn-out sock. It was a calm and quiet part of town—quiet like abandoned. A few down-and-outs lay on benches in the shade of palm trees, but there was no other sign of life. On the far side of the park was a large square and the centre of it was occupied by an enormous, blank-walled church. High up there was a balcony that went all round the building with windows giving on to it, coloured glass alternating with plain. There was a spire, a canopy leading to the main door and a huge notice along the biggest wall:

THE CHURCH OF GOD'S WILL:
THE REVEREND J. TURRILL
JOIN THE FIGHT AGAINST EVIL

The girl drew the car up to the canopy. She pulled on the handbrake but did not switch off the motor.

"On my own?" I asked.

"Yes," she said.

I got out of the car and slammed the door. "What do I do?"

"Just go in and ask for the Reverend."

"Will I see you again?"

The girl pushed the gear lever into first. "No," she said, "you won't." And the car leapt forward, picked up speed and disappeared round the nearest corner.

Above the church door was a remote control camera watching me. I pressed a button and there was a buzz and a click. A voice said, "Enter," and the door sprang open. I went in and found myself in a small, intimate chapel whose size bore no relation to the huge building I had seen from the outside.

In front of me were two separate rows of benches divided by an aisle which led to an altar—a solid block of white marble—and above it a massive wooden crucifix on a yellow stone wall; no windows but a lectern on a raised platform, nothing more. I coughed and walked forward. The place smelt damp after the sunshine; a carpet deadened my footsteps.

As I neared the altar a man in a dark suit came from behind it. He was a tall man with strong thighs and a face that was circular and topped by a crust of solid blond hair. His pink hands, though holding each other as gently as they would holy relics, looked capable of anything.

"Yes," he said, and his voice sounded like extreme unction.

"I've come to see the Reverend."

"Is your need spiritual?"

"I hope not."

The acolyte nodded. "Follow me," he said.

Behind the altar was an entry which gave on to a passage which in turn led to the very rear of the building. On either side of this passage were doors, about a dozen in all, and every one of them was closed. At the end of the passage we came to two flights of stairs—one up, one down—and we went up.

The staircase was narrow. At the top of maybe twenty steps was a landing and guarding it were two more of the Reverend's angels. As I had now come to expect they sported well-cut suits, strong shoulders and seraphic faces with the bright light of true religion blazing through their skins from somewhere a long way off.

These guards did not seem to see me as my guide conducted me past them and out onto the second floor of the church. Here the whole length and breadth of the building was occupied by open plan offices, each one surrounded by low partitions that separated it from its neighbours.

This was the hub of the Reverend's world and there were scores of dedicated people running it for him, talking to each other, answering phones and working computer terminals. Like the guards, every one of them was lit from within, animated and healthy looking.

I followed the acolyte through the twists and turns of the offices and stopped, when he stopped, near the end of one of the windowless walls. My companion pressed a button and suddenly there was a small lift, small as a coffin. He motioned me inside and in I went, half-expecting him to follow. He did not. The door closed and I was on my own.

I was in there just long enough to get scared—the steel door seemed air-tight and there was no ventilation grille. I could feel no movement but when the door opened I was certainly in a different place. I stepped out and found myself in a magical blaze of sunshine and colour.

At first my sight, and my other senses also, were dazed and I could see nothing. Then I could see. I was in a large room that must have occupied at least half the area enclosed by the four walls of the church, and here were the windows I'd noticed from the street, tall and wide and opening onto the balcony. Every alternate window was clear and the ones in between were made of modern stained glass, the colours exquisitely chosen—blue and crimson, green and gold, just like a cathedral.

At the top of the room was a desk I could have played snooker on. Behind it sat the Reverend, the power still beaming out of him in solid shafts of light, while the colour from the windows lent a heavenly glow to the outline of his face. He was a saint, still incandescent from his contact with the other world.

Here and there about the room, but widely separated from each other, were more desks with a couple of women at each of them—the kind of women the Reverend seemed to like: Californian and beautiful, good enough to leave home for and as big as football players.

Underfoot was a white carpet, thick and seamless, and standing on it, all over, in no particular order, like unwanted chess-pieces, were some of the Reverend's large men, suits and faces as before. They did not move but stared at me, their hands held loosely before them.

I hesitated and then stepped into the room, trudging

across the acres of floor. Still no one moved save the Reverend, who rose and came from behind his desk, advancing towards me on seven-league feet. Again I saw how massive he was, yet how well proportioned. His white and even teeth smiled in his tanned face. He looked so clean, his hair freshly washed, his clothes perfect. As we met, all eyes in the room were on us for a second, then everyone looked away—the women working at their desks, the men waiting to be called.

I came into the Reverend's shadow and he took me by the elbow, the pressure of the fingers only gentle though I felt helpless as soon as he touched me. I turned as the Reverend turned me and I went with him onto the balcony and we looked down into the empty square and over the park and the palm trees, away into the layer of dark brown smog that lay under the bitter sunshine of Los Angeles.

"I'm glad you came," said the Reverend, his voice as gentle and as strong as his touch. "But I thought you might."

I swallowed. "I really don't know what's going on," I said, "that's why I came, to tell you that."

The Reverend exerted a little more pressure on my elbow and we began to walk, side by side, along the balcony.

"Tell me what you have to say."

"There is nothing to say," I insisted. "I'm a free-lance film technician. I've never been to Los Angeles before. I'm not even religious."

The Reverend nodded. "How did you come to be chosen?"

"The cameraman chose me. The assistant he was going to bring with him had an accident. I only had two days to get ready."

"An accident." It was not a question.

"He got run over. He was dead before they could get him to hospital."

"Yes, we know. Did he telephone you at any time?"

"No . . . there was no reason for him to. He didn't know I existed." The balcony turned a corner and so did we. The view had changed now. Not far away I could see six lanes of traffic on a freeway. It was all strangely quiet. A plane glinted in the sky.

The Reverend stopped and leant against the wall of the church and gazed over the city as if it were a possession of his and he could give it away if he wanted. I looked down. It was a long way and the ironwork balustrade was low. The square was empty except for the Reverend's black limousine.

"I don't know whether I can believe you," he said. "Ten million dollars is a great temptation."

"Ten million dollars," I said, moving back from the balcony's edge. "I'm not in that league. What would I do with ten million dollars?"

The Reverend did not even bother to answer such a stupid question. He moved on and I followed him, keeping close to the wall of the church and passing windows now which were small and where curtains fluttered.

"Your predecessor in London, Rapps . . . I think he might have been killed because he was trying to be too clever. He may have been trying to come to an arrangement with those who do not love my church and they killed him, when the arrangement didn't work, mainly to stop the money from reaching me. For that they would do anything."

The Reverend stopped abruptly and turned and I almost bumped into him. We were now standing by an open window and I saw a large sitting room, richly appointed. "But

Rapps had been reliable for years. Whenever he was unable to come himself he sent someone else, someone just like you, a replacement."

"The people who killed him," I cried, my voice cracking with hope like an adolescent's. "It's obvious, they've got your money."

The Reverend sighed. "They would only have killed Rapps as a last resort—to stop the money from getting to me. Had it been in their possession already they would not have bothered. They are not amateurs. They have been hired because they are the best."

"The best?"

"That is why they searched you all at Newport. They also searched your hotel rooms while you were away . . . you didn't notice?"

"You mean those Mexicans at Newport, you mean they killed Rapps because they didn't find what they were looking for?"

The Reverend set off again. "I think so. And they will kill you too if they think it will stop the money getting to me."

"I didn't know Rapps was bringing you money," I said. "I just brought the gear over." I was struck by a sudden idea. "It was impounded by customs, you know. The money could have been taken then."

The Reverend smiled at my innocence. "That is how it is done. My men went through your luggage inch by inch. Rapps always delivered the money that way. This time things have gone wrong. This time, perhaps, the temptation was too much."

"One of the others on the film crew," I suggested, "like the producer or the director. It must be one of them."

The Reverend stopped and folded his arms. We were

back outside the window he'd brought me through. "I am never wrong about people," he said. "It is a feeling I get. One of you has ten million dollars of mine and I think it is you. If it is one of the others, then it is for you to discover which one of them it is. Whatever happens you will not leave the country until I have what I want. My son, the forces of evil wish to destroy me and my work. This is not simply money we are discussing here . . . we are talking of the salvation of this very church and the people in it. How long does your filming continue?"

"About a week more."

"Then you have that week. I shall be as patient as that, but I warn you: do not try to leave the country or even the state. It will not work, nor will a visit to the Los Angeles police force. There is nowhere for you to go. I do not wish to do you harm but my church means more than any individual alive . . . or dead."

"But the money must be in a packing-case. Ten million dollars, you can't hide ten million dollars."

"You can if it has been converted into diamonds of the finest quality," said the Reverend, and he stepped back into the great reception room.

Nothing in the room had changed. The women were at their places, the men stood, statuesque, waiting. I went to run after the Reverend but he was already halfway to his desk and two of his men moved between us and steered me towards the lift. I was finished with for the time being.

I hardly knew what I was doing after that. The lift descended. I followed where I was led, down the stairs and into the basement. Two other men were on either side of me. My throat went dry. My hands shook. I was convinced that I was to be beaten up, slowly and scientifically, down below the street where my voice could not be heard, but the Reverend was not like that.

One of the acolytes unlocked a door and threw it open. I was pushed to the threshold, to blink in the hard light of a bare bulb.

The room was the size of a small prison cell, but it was not clean and there was no bed. On the floor was a naked man, his body covered in sores, his hair growing in tufts. I could not see his face for his head was cradled in his arms and he rocked himself sideways and back, sideways and back, crooning senselessly to himself. He was not aware of the door opening or of me standing looking down at him. The smell of the room made my stomach contract and a sweat broke out all over me.

"Take a good look," said one of the men, and he pulled me away, back along the corridor.

I felt very ill then and was not aware of walking any more. I suppose the men escorting me simply placed a hand under each of my arms and half-carried me up the stairs and through the chapel. The outside air was no relief either. As I came into it, my lungs burned with its heat and its heavy charge of exhaust fumes.

Waiting for me was the great stretch automobile I had seen from above. This close it seemed even more threatening, gleaming black and chrome, dazzling in the sun. I was frightened. I stiffened my legs and struggled like a child against the grip that held me.

"What are you doing?" I said. "Please leave me alone. Let me take a cab. Leave me alone."

"Take it easy," said a voice. "The Reverend just wants you back at the hotel, safe and sound. It's the least he can do. He is a very good man, you know." And with this I was propelled away from the hot sunshine and into the gloom of an air-conditioned climate. The door clicked behind me and the car moved away from the kerb.

Travelling in the stretch was like being driven around in a house. The main bench seat was as big as a double bed and there were enough fold-away armchairs to furnish a preview theatre. There was also a television set, a radio-telephone and a drinks cabinet. I needed a drink so I poured myself a large brandy and put a handful of ice in it.

As I relaxed, the green light on the telephone began winking and I looked away from it. It couldn't be for me. Then the instrument began to make a low, buzzing noise as well so I answered it. I could always say the Reverend was out.

It was the Reverend.

"Our church does as much as it can," said his friendly voice, "to help those who have been destroyed by the power of drugs, but there is little we can do when their fate has already been decided. You can perhaps see now that death is not always the worst that life has to offer. How lucky you are not to be addicted to such substances . . . though you should know that if such a thing did happen to you . . . and it can happen to anyone . . . we would take you into our care and do everything we could to cure you . . . Unfortunately, not everyone can be saved."

The line went dead and I replaced the receiver. I tried to laugh but the noise came out like the cackle of a madman. I should have been able to laugh, for there was much to laugh at: the colours in that great room above the church, the angels and acolytes waiting on their leader's every word, the holy dread in which the Reverend was held. This car even. Everything was over the top and should have been ripe for derision—but how could I deride such things when everyone around me was taking them so seriously.

I gulped at my brandy and shivered. It was cold in the car. I felt ill again. I was going to have to do something. I leant forward to reach the air-conditioning control and switched it to warm.

6

Went the Day Well?

The stretch took me back to Treetops and I had lunch sent to my room. I didn't see any of the others and I didn't want to. They were all out anyway and a note in my pigeon hole told me that we wouldn't be shooting until the following morning.

After I'd eaten I changed into bathing trunks and went over to the swimming-pool and found Angela on a sun-lounger. I was glad to see her; she understood this crazy town.

She put down her book and smiled from behind her sunglasses. Most of her was brown and only a few little bits of white peeped out from behind her bikini. I sat down, dropping my towel and my magazine onto the ground. There were two other people by the pool but they were out of earshot, reclining in the shade of a eucalyptus.

"Where have you been?" asked Angela. "The others said you'd gone off with some girl."

"She told me she was horning her way through college. Was that a line?"

"They do it, lots of them. I knew an elementary school teacher who did it."

"This girl took me to a place. Do you know anything about it—the Church of God's Will?" Then I told her what had happened to me. I had to tell someone and at least she didn't laugh.

Angela pulled a lever and her sun-lounger raised her into a sitting position. She looked at me seriously. "Not many people from outside get to see the Reverend," she said. "That's something of an honour. He's a powerful man, that I know. I used to free-lance for the Los Angeles *Times* and I once saw a feature they did . . . on him . . . only it never got to be published. The truth about him is hard to come by."

"He thinks I'm someone else, thinks I've got these diamonds. He made my blood freeze."

"All you can do is tell him what you know."

"That's just it. I don't know anything. It could be anyone else on this unit. Tony, for example. He knew this other assistant, this Rapps. They've worked together before."

A shadow fell over my shoulder and a Mexican waiter in a red jacket leant over me. "A drink, señor?" he asked.

"A beer and a Coke," I said, and the Mexican went away as silently as he'd come. "They're creepy, these waiters."

Angela stood suddenly. "Yes, they are." She stepped to the edge of the pool and dived in. I watched her swim away from me, her long body hardly disturbing the water, golden against the rippling blue of the tiles. At the end of the pool she turned and swam back, climbed the steps and dripped water over my legs as she settled herself on her sun-lounger again.

"You ever heard of Hassan Sabor, the Old Man of the Mountain?"

I shook my head.

"He lived in a castle at the end of a green valley in the

middle of a desert somewhere. He used to get these guys and drug them up to the eye-balls with marijuana, hashish they called it. Then he'd have them carried into these beautiful gardens with fountains pouring wine, and beautiful maidens ready to do their every bidding. That's right. Then, after a few days, he'd have them brought back again and he'd tell 'em they'd seen paradise and when they died that's where they'd end up, sure and certain.

"Then the Old Man of the Mountain would send messages to the local kings and ask for money and such, and if they didn't oblige he'd send one of his boys along in the middle of the night and when the king woke he might find a dagger in his throat . . . so people used to pay. These guys were called hashshashin . . . that's where the word comes from . . . assassins."

"I never knew."

"Some people say the Reverend's a little like that, but that's only the people who don't like what he does. Most people think what he does is good."

"Like what?"

"When he came into town about twenty years ago he started these self-help groups. People used to go to his place and stay there for weeks and he'd investigate their personalities right down to the bone . . . then he'd build them up again. Real no-hopers, people who'd thrown in the towel. He'd help them back on their feet and give them a glimpse of paradise, make them believe in themselves. Hundreds of them. And they never left. They worship him, no I mean it. So he founded the church and they stayed and it gets bigger all the time. There's nothing else like it in the whole state. There's a whole village out in the hills, with a farm to grow the food. A beautiful place, they say. I met some of them once, seemed like good people."

"The ones I saw looked at him like he was some mega-movie-star—all the time."

"They believe in him, Del. He's got a hospital in the church, you know. He takes junkies off the street and helps them back. No wonder they worship him."

Again the Mexican appeared behind me. He placed the drinks on a table, took my room number and disappeared as soundlessly as before.

"Did Tony see the police about those Mexicans at Newport the other night?"

Angela reached for her Coke. "He did, and the fuzz wrote it all down and said it happened all the time. The only thing that surprised them was that no one got hurt. They think you were mistaken for some rival gang and the Mexicans were trying to warn you to stay off their territory."

"Well, the Reverend's got me down for something. He thinks I have his diamonds and if the Mexicans find out what he's thinking they'll do to me what they did to Rapps."

Angela laid a hand on my knee; her touch was icy from holding the glass of Coke. "You're going to need the Reverend on your side," she said. "He's the only one who can protect you. But it's simple. All you have to do is tell him the truth."

"That's the problem," I said. "The truth is what no one wants to hear."

Back in my room I closed the sliding window and drew the heavy curtains. Next I took the bottle of whisky from the fridge and poured myself a large one.

I didn't like much of what Angela had told me. Convincing the Reverend he was mistaken didn't look too easy a job. Ten million dollars was a lot of money and nobody on earth was going to take a stranger's word on such a subject.

Then there were the others: the Mexicans. If they came to believe that I was a replacement for Rapps, or even just privy to an actual or imagined double-cross of his—the stealing of the diamonds—then they would push me over the edge if only to keep things tidy. Like the proverb said, I had two chances: "A dog's chance or no chance." Either the Mexicans got me or I ended up being "cured" in the Reverend's hospital. If I went to the police they would write it all down and tell me not to worry—it was just a simple case of mistaken identity. And so it was, but it was a mistake that could have very serious consequences—mainly for me.

I groaned and rolled over the bed and picked up the telephone. I wanted to talk to someone; I wanted to go home and hide under the bed.

As soon as my wife answered I knew it had been a mistake. What could I say? Somebody thought I had ten million dollars of theirs and might turn me into a drug addict if I didn't pay up. After a story like that she'd think me even less worthy of consideration than she normally did.

"Jesus, Del," she said, "it's two in the morning." She was what they used to call well-spoken, and the sound of her voice rattled down from the satellite like a bone china cup and saucer. Even on a clear day her parents couldn't see the tracks I came from the other side of.

"I thought I might come home early," I said. "I'm fed up with it."

She came awake then. "Listen, Del, don't start walking

off the job. You haven't had any work for months and we need it."

"It's not that . . ."

She wasn't listening and the delay of the signal bouncing up and over the hemisphere gave her just the right amount of breathing time.

"Only a few more days. It was four months without any work, remember, under my feet watching videos. No thanks."

"The kids all right?"

"We've been burgled too, as if I didn't have enough on my mind. I had to have the police in."

"Burgled?"

". . . but they weren't any good. They couldn't understand why nothing had been taken, not even your video machine. I knew. It was because none of our so-called possessions are worth having."

"Was anything taken?"

". . . but the children thought it was a lark . . . and there haven't been any phone calls for work . . ."

"Were there any phone calls?"

". . . though these two men came round to see you. Talked to me a great deal. They wanted to know if I thought you'd be interested in a feature being shot in Brazil next year. They wanted to know a lot about you. Whether you could stand the jungle, what kind of person you were, that kind of thing . . ."

"What did they want to know?"

". . . anyway you wouldn't want to do it so what's the point? They gave a fiver each to the kids but I took it away from them and put it towards the house-keeping, which reminds me you'd better ask Matrix to send me a cheque on your salary . . . I need it. I had to borrow from my

father last week. I don't have to tell you what he
said . . ."

"I will," I said, "I'll go and do it right away." And I put
the receiver down before my words had time to reach their
destination. Even a worm like me becomes used to having
nowhere to turn.

Next morning after breakfast I backed the station-wagon
out of the car park and up to the gear, which was piled in a
sprawling heap outside the entrance of our pavilion. Ernie
and Nick were waiting for me and as I manoeuvred the car
into position Nick opened the tail-gate. While we were
doing this Alex appeared, running down an open stairway.
He was dressed like the rest of us in shorts and sneakers
and a sports shirt. Ronnie came, more slowly, behind him.

"There's no Deegan," he said, "just pick-ups."

"What I want this morning," said Alex, "is some gen-
eral views of L.A., and some shots from the car, but we'll
go up to Griffiths Park first, for a view of the city and that
Hollywood sign . . . you know?"

Nick and I loaded the gear, and as we finished, Angela
drove up in her Beetle convertible. "Hi, you guys," she
said. "Give you a lift?"

Before anyone else could answer I had slipped into the
car with her and closed the door. The others found this
haste of mine very amusing but I didn't care. It wasn't
often that I got to be driven around by a good-looking
woman. I needed it, they didn't.

Driving back and forth up the zig-zags of the road that led
to the Observatory in Griffiths Park we could see, below
us, the skyscrapers of Century City glittering in the
golden-grey air with the sun filtering through a death-deal-

ing haze. And far away towards the invisible horizon, on the distant freeways, the traffic moved unceasingly—six lanes in each direction, solid lines, like bugs in a bloodstream.

At the top we got out of the cars and looked over the city.

"Put it here," said Ernie.

I took the tripod from the station-wagon and set the camera on it, cleaned it and loaded a magazine. All around us parked cars, bearing number plates from every state in the union, shimmered in the sun. Tourists walked by us and smiled at our accents. Alex wore a dark blue baseball hat, monogrammed with a big *T* for Treetops Golf Club.

"Right," he said. "I want a slow pan right across the city."

I stared at him. Was it he who had taken Rapps's place? Had he been asked to bring the diamonds in and then been tempted by so much money? It was possible. He looked man enough for the job. Short and stocky, broad in the shoulder with a jutting jaw half-covered with a beard like a rusty wire brush.

He caught me studying him and narrowed his eyes suspiciously, trying to work out what I was thinking. I broke my gaze from his and moved the camera to a different angle under Ernie's direction. "It's better here," he said.

"After that," continued Alex, following us to the new position, "I want another pan, a hundred and eighty degrees, then you'll zoom into the sign over there on the hill."

Nick came over, carrying his Nagra. "Do you want an atmos track on this?" he asked.

I turned and looked at the sign. It was the famous one that was on all the postcards, big with separate white letters as wide and as tall as four men maybe. HOLLYWOOD it read, standing out sharply against the dark green of the hillside.

"It's awfully tatty," said Ronnie. "The *D*'s lop-sided and there's an effigy hanging from it." He was looking through binoculars and I noticed that he had a bandage round his right hand.

"What's wrong with your hand?" I asked him.

"I had a row with Tony last night, about money."

"Not ten million dollars' worth?"

Ronnie looked at me as if I were crazy. "That's a feature budget," he said. "If we had money like that we wouldn't be shooting this crap, would we? No, just about expenses. But you can't win with Tony. I got so wound up I punched the wall."

"The wall?"

"If I hadn't punched the wall I'd have punched him and he's a lot bigger than me."

Alex suddenly pushed between us. "I know it's tatty," he said. "If you'd stop yacking about it maybe you could find time to get over there and straighten it up, take the effigy down."

"There's been a protest about the sign falling apart," said Angela. "That's what the effigy is. It was on the radio this morning."

Tony went towards Angela's car. "Come on, Ange," he said, "drive me over there."

"Why don't we do a couple of pan shots," said Ernie, "while we're waiting."

Alex watched Tony and Angela get into her Beetle and drive away. "Okay," he said, "why don't we?"

Ernie did a shot and then did another two or three to make sure. The sky over Los Angeles dreamed away like a soft Neapolitan ice. A blanket of gold blazed across the stratosphere, fading along its under edge into pale blue. Lower down it became darker, until at last, hiding the feet of the skyscrapers, the brown smog rose to grapple with the air, climbing a third of the way up the mad glitter of Century City.

Alex swore. "I thought it was supposed to be clearer up here." He dabbed an eye. "This bloody smog—I can't stop crying."

"It's this film," said Ernie. "It would make anyone weep."

I moved away. Alex looked cornered. This was going to be one of his bad days. "Look, Ernie," he said, "just switch on the camera when I tell you, and the rest of the time you shut up."

"Wait a minute." Ronnie got between Alex and Ernie, his fox-face creased with anxiety. "This is ridiculous. It's this smog. It gets to your nervous system. I'm sure it does, until you get used to it."

"You get used to it," said Ernie, "because I won't."

Ronnie raised his bandaged hand like a glove-puppet. "Look at this. I wouldn't normally do a thing like this. It's the smog."

Nick took the binoculars from the roof of the limousine and looked towards the sign. "Strewth," he said, after a moment. "There's a lot of cars up there now. Flashing lights and everything, must be the fuzz."

Alex snatched the binoculars from Nick and raised them to his eyes. "We can't shoot it now, there's cops all over it. We might as well wrap it here."

I took the camera off the sticks and packed it away in its case. Then I collapsed the tripod and put it and the battery into the station-wagon.

As we waited, Angela's Beetle sped up the hill, slid round a couple of hairpin bends and eventually came to a stop beside us. Tony leant out of the window, his eyes bright with mirth.

"It was lousy with cops," he said, "and they're very touchy about that sign. There's been a lot of trouble about it."

Alex whined. "Today of all days, just when I want some shots of it."

"Well, you can forget it." Tony was sniggering. "You see that effigy wasn't an effigy at all; they took that down this morning. This was a real human-being hanging from the *D.*"

"Really," cried Alex, suddenly joyful. He grabbed the binoculars. "Suicide?"

"No," said Tony, laughing again, "no it wasn't."

Angela raised her face from a contemplation of her hands on the driving wheel. She looked at me mournfully.

"No it wasn't," she said. "It was one of those damn Mexicans, and his hands were tied behind his back."

7

There's No Business Like Show Business

The three cars drove in slow procession through the Santa Monica mountains. The roads were summery and we were on our way back to Treetops, tired. It had been a long hot day.

"We'll have champagne tonight," said Alex when we were unloading at the hotel. "Ice cold."

Ernie and Nick helped me carry the gear to my room and we stacked it inside. I gave them a beer each from the fridge and they sat on the beds while I unloaded the magazines in the changing bag.

"Can't we get out on our own," I said. "We need a rest from the others."

"Not tonight we won't," said Ernie. "Alex and Tony have got ladies coming to dinner so it's a pound to a penny they'll want both the cars to move 'em around."

"What about that dead Mexican this morning? What about that?"

Ernie shrugged his shoulders. "You heard what the cops told Tony. There's some gang war going on, nothing to do with us."

"Hell of a coincidence, isn't it? I mean Newport and now this."

Ernie shrugged again. "We'll be out of here in a few days, then it'll be just a traveller's tale."

"Coincidence or not," said Nick, throwing his empty beer can into the bin, "it was horrible, that guy hanging there like that."

When the two of them had gone I took a shower and put on some clean clothes. Then, as soon as I was ready I set out for the bar, following a line of paving stones across the grass and passing between the bushes and trees. The rabbits and chipmunks watched me as I went by, hoping for food. They were disappointed. Along by the side of the ornamental lake, on the near side from the links, I found two golf balls and slipped them into my pocket. I thought the kids might like them when I got home.

As usual it was dark and air-conditioned in the bar and I was the first one there. I ordered myself a white wine and sat on a stool facing the main entrance. It was a big room with alcoves all round the walls, a dance floor in the middle and chairs and tables filling the rest of the available space. Some nights it doubled up as a disco and on those nights they played the music loud enough to vibrate the clothes off your back.

I crunched a lump of ice and thought about Rapps, moving three ideas around in my mind. The most likely scenario was that Rapps had been planning to disappear with the diamonds all along, having converted them back into cash so that he'd be ready to make a run for it as soon as it suited him. In which event the likeliest place for the money to be hidden was in a numbered account in Geneva.

On the other hand if Rapps had become aware that the Mexicans were on his tail, he might have tried to do a deal with them. When the deal hadn't worked out, he'd refused to hand the diamonds over and he'd been killed to prevent the money getting to the Reverend.

But there was a third possibility. Rapps might have had no intention at all of double-crossing the Reverend, and realising that things were getting dangerous, he'd given the diamonds to someone else to bring over—some unknown who'd not yet arrived or, more probably, someone else on the unit.

It certainly wasn't me; that much I knew. Deegan was already a millionaire; Ernie and Nick didn't have the style and Ronnie was a coward in the same league as I was. That left only Alex and Tony, and Tony was the one I had marked down on my card, mainly because I liked him least of anyone on the location. But more than that, he looked the most probable, with his too handsome face and his too confident eyes. It made sense. Tony would sell his mother into a Peruvian whore-house for ten dollars. With ten million he could found an empire, produce his own movies. Alone amongst us he was the only one with enough gall to steal the money, and the only one with the appetite to spend it. Tony Maretta was the man.

"You like another drink?" The Mexican barman stood ready, his hands on the top of the counter, a big bandit smile under his moustache. These guys were everywhere, growing out of the ground like toadstools.

"Yeah," I said. "Do you come over the border every morning?"

"Please?" he said.

"A white wine."

"And a beer," said Ernie, getting onto a stool.

"And a scotch," said Nick. "I feel like getting drunk."

"I'll join you," I said, and put some money on the

counter. "Ernie, this Phil Rapps, did you work with him much?"

"Yeah, though not all the time. He was always pretty busy, worked a lot over here, and for Dutch television."

"Amsterdam," I said, "diamonds. Those Mexicans at Newport could have been looking for Rapps. I bet his getting run over wasn't an accident."

Ernie looked at Nick and they both laughed. "In Los Angeles," Ernie said, "they have a murder every six hours —gangs, territories; Italians, Puerto Ricans, Apaches even. A Mexican getting killed out here is one thing. Rapps getting run over outside Ickenham underground station is another. I ask you, murder in Ickenham . . . it doesn't even sound right."

In the restaurant the candles were lit and the light was golden and the furniture was brown. The tablecloths were crisp and beige and everywhere the glasses were shining. We had a large table and Deegan sat with Millie at the head of it. Next to him, on the other side, was a Hollywood theatrical agent who'd invited himself along to talk about work; then came Alex and Tony and the others.

"These women," said Nick as he took a seat on my right, below the salt, "I heard Alex talking about them. They've come to discuss some script. I bet they think Tony's some big-time producer and Alex is Louis Malle. Everyone's on the make in this town."

In that setting the two women looked mature and glamorous with gleaming hair as solid and as grainy as polished wood. Two lovely heads: one of bronze, the other of gold.

"Wigs," said Angela, her voice turning like a screwdriver.

"Their names are Kate and Kim," said Ernie as he

opened a menu as big as the Domesday Book, "or is it Kim and Kate?"

Kim and Kate had well-organised features, unwrinkled by time. They weren't young and they weren't old and I never knew which one was which. They wore magnificent long skirts, skirts of a touchable soft stuff that was cut on the cross and swirled like water between their lithe Californian legs. Every time Kate or Kim crossed her thighs, there was a swish of luxury and warmth that made my groin ache.

Tony and Alex had been collecting fashionable American clothes for these evenings and they looked as smooth and as stately as marble columns. Tony was a smile that went on for ever, a big easy smile like a mask on a stick. I watched him closely, wanting to learn, even at my age, though I knew it was too late for me.

Tony Maretta had always got what he wanted. He had grown up to take the good things of life for granted: women, travel, cars, money. I, by comparison, had come to manhood with envy in my heart and contempt on my face. What little I'd got I'd got sitting at other people's tables, tables like this one. Nobody like me could touch Tony. If ten million dollars fell into his lap he'd just naturally think it was his. Me, I'd scream and run away.

He caught me watching him and smiled, indicating Kim with his fork. "She's got a twelve-year-old son," he said proudly, appropriating for himself the son and the act of birth in one sentence. "Imagine that."

At last two Mexicans came, bearing iced water, and then the waitress took the order. "I'll just have whatever he has," I said, and pointed at Tony. The service that evening was unhurried and so we drank champagne while we waited. The noise level at the table began to rise and as it rose we shouted. It was lobster first, with Alaskan crab claws. After a while the waitress returned, cleared the table and laid more dishes before us: New York steaks, brochettes of lamb and Hungarian goulash.

I was still drinking champagne when the reds and whites arrived and I hurried to catch up, spilling wine on my chin. I saw Angela raise her hands to the nape of her neck, loosening her hair so that it fell around her face, making her lovely. And Kim and Kate seized their *canard au poivre vert* with their hands and lifted large lumps of it to their mouths, kissing the meat, and the dark gravy dripped from their purple lips and stained their teeth and tongues.

I closed my eyes and opened them again. Nick was talking into the ear of a waitress. I admired the curve of her back as she bent to listen. She had thick ropes of hair and I knew that when she turned to face me she would be beautiful. Why were they all so wonderful? Why were they all so tall? Had it all been designed on purpose to make me feel as masterful as a randy sparrow?

The sounds changed and the lights began to strobe, pulling at my retinas. We had moved to an alcove in the disco. Alex's head hung over our table, raw, like a long side of beef, gazing with deep meaning into Kate's face. I saw Deegan standing at the bar with Millie, and the Hollywood agent was slumped, happy in his corner, his eyes opaque with a smoky joy. He stared sightlessly at the dancers as they moved together in the deep well of the dance floor, like lava in a dark pit. Without turning his head to see if I was there or not he passed me a joint and I smoked it all and began to float above the room like a spirit called to a Ouija board: "I bring you a message from the other side . . . Phil Rapps here . . . ten million dollars is okay, but it ain't worth dying for. Beware of the Church of God's Will."

Time began to spread itself and become endless, then it shrivelled and disappeared. I got up to leave the table and staggered into Tony, who was whispering into Kim's wig. "I'll get that script off the ground—you see if I don't."

I stumbled away in the direction of the restaurant, where the lavatories were. More large girls were marching into the disco now, freed from the day's work, arms linked, two by two, thrusting me out of their way.

Angela put an arm round me and led me onto the dance floor. I leant into her. "You're so lovely," I said. "Did you know that?"

Before she could answer, I was on my own again but I could see our table and Ernie and Nick were there, the Hollywood agent too, slumping even lower. As I sat down, Nick hit me with his elbow. "I've got the waitress coming," he said, peering anxiously into the sweat and the noise. "She is coming, you know. She said she was, after work, as soon . . ."

Then Nick was gone, before the end of his sentence, or perhaps long after I'd finished listening to it.

"Where's Maretta?" I asked Ernie.

"Where d'yer think?"

"And Deegan?"

"Same place."

I got up and set off for the lavatories again. On the way I bumped into one of the Mexican waiters. It was my fault but he was the one to say "sorry." I caught him by the arm and held on. "It's not me," I said, "you know, it's not me, it's Maretta, Tony Maretta. He's the only one of us who would know what to do with ten million dollars."

I leant my forehead against the sweating tiles and emptied my bladder. I had drunk so much—much too much. I ran the tap over my head, rubbed my scalp and then contemplated myself in the mirror. How long had I been away from the disco? Was it time for me to go to bed? Nick appeared beside me, his face angry.

"Where have you been?" I asked, and looked at my watch though I couldn't read it.

"I've been over to that waitress's place. She's got an apartment on the other side of the golf club. We got into this waterbed."

"Waterbed. How long have you been away?"

"I dunno, about an hour or two."

"Into a waterbed."

"Yeah, and out of it. I'm so bloody angry, what a waste of time."

"How do you mean? How the hell did she get you out of a waterbed once you'd got into it?"

"Easy . . . just as I'm getting through the preliminaries, she rolled over and said, 'You older men are all the same, you only want one thing.'"

"Older men," I said, "but you're only thirty odd. How old is she?"

"I don't know, eighteen. What do young men want then? Intellectual conversation?"

"What happened?"

"What do you think happened. It went down so fast it looked like last night's party balloon. Older men!"

"That's the trouble, being handsome," I said, showing my pleasure a little too eagerly. "When a girl goes to bed with someone old and ugly like me I know it's got to be because of my wonderful personality and nothing else because there isn't anything else."

I hadn't realized Nick was so upset. "Piss off, why don't

you?" he said, "you bloody know-all joker." He brushed by me and went out through the door, leaving it to swing in my face as I tried to follow him.

Outside, when I got there, the warm night air wrapped itself around my head like a wet towel. I blinked and the blinking made me stumble. I headed for the steps that led to the gardens. Somewhere on the other side of the trees and bushes I would find my bedroom.

I staggered a little on the rolling ground but I felt content. The squirrels, rabbits and chipmunks were asleep in the dark but the cool starlight was reflected like a spray of tinsel along the edge of the lake and the moon was clear of all cloud. It was peaceful, and after the noise of the disco the silence was soothing. The Reverend and his world seemed a universe away. It was good to get drunk.

Then I heard a sound in the bushes and my contentment evaporated. I stopped, convinced that I was to be knifed. I crouched to the ground and kept still. It might be anyone —the Reverend's men, the Mexicans. Or a mugger—out here people were killed for a few dollars on their own motel verandahs. I felt in my pockets. One twenty-dollar bill was all I had. I took it out and held it up in front of me, like a cross before a vampire, but ready to relinquish it.

The noise came again. I put the twenty between my teeth, got on my hands and knees and began to creep away. Then I relaxed. The noise was someone being violently sick. I peered forward and saw a shape leaning against a tree. The shape was sick again, a deep retching sound that told me the stomach was empty. I rose to my feet and slipped the twenty back into my pocket.

"Are you all right, Nick? It's Del."

"Too bloody old, that's how I am, too bloody old at thirty." He was almost crying.

"Oh shut up, Nick. I'm forty already and that's worse. Nobody wants to be old."

"Aw, let's get away from here, it smells of sick."

"Don't worry. The squirrels will have it in the morning."

We put our arms round each other and lurched down a slope which led to the side of the lake. There was no noise from anywhere and the ordered landscape was deserted.

"I'm going for a swim," said Nick, and I noticed that he wore a hotel towel round his neck.

"Good idea," I said, and began to remove my clothes.

In a second Nick was naked, tanned all over except for the soft band of white across his buttocks. He flailed his way forward and dived, an arcing body. He swam two or three strokes and then got to his feet, the water rising to his chest.

"Come on, chicken," he called, "it's great!" Then without warning his body folded in two and his head submerged, his cry of pain going under the surface with him.

I whimpered. "My God," I said, and rushed to the water's edge, where I hesitated then walked into the lake, hands outstretched. What could have done for him? A heart attack? I thought of running to the disco for assistance; after all I was no swimmer.

I took a deep breath and bobbed under the water like a little girl on her first visit to the seaside. I groped around and came up for air. Nick was standing a couple of yards away from me, looking pleased with himself.

"Did you get cramp?" I asked.

"Cramp be buggered," said Nick. "I trod on one of

them damn golf balls, right in the middle of my foot and I fell over and went looking for it. Here it is."

He showed me the ball against the stars and a moment later, with all his strength, he hurled it high into the sky. We listened and my teeth chattered. After a long while in the air the ball landed with a crashing of glass; there was a gleam of white in the darkness as Nick grinned.

"I got a windscreen in the car park," he announced.

"Vandalism in Los Angeles is allowed," I said, and waded out of the lake. While I dried myself on the towel, Nick swam up and down once or twice then joined me on the shore.

"The towel's soaking," he said. "I'm going to bed. If anyone asks about the windscreen, we'll say we're Australian. That's how they get their bad name, you know. It's not them really, it's all the English saying they're them."

We dressed and went together through the trees in the direction of our pavilion car park, searching without success for the shattered windscreen. After a moment or two more Nick left me and I stretched out on a bench under a eucalyptus, lacking the energy to go to my room, enjoying the quiet of the night for a little longer. I felt slightly sick now and my head was far from clear. Gradually the starlight paled and the black line of the surrounding hills detached itself from the sky. The world was empty and beautiful.

I was asleep when the film unit limousine bounced over the ramps from the highway and drove along the hotel road to reach our pavilion. I came properly awake as the car halted silently, and I waited and watched for someone to get out of it. But no one did and I wondered why Tony didn't take her to his room, but then again there are people who like doing it in cars and perhaps he was one of them.

While I listened to the noises another, bigger car came in from the highway and headed towards me, switching off its headlights as it advanced. I was not visible on the bench but nevertheless I got up and went to stand behind a tree, hiding myself in the dark tent of its drooping lower branches. Above the hills the grey sky was warming into pink and the dawn was not far away.

The car stopped and eight men got out at once. Big men. They went straight to the limousine, flung open the rear doors and pulled Tony and Kim out into the open. It was light enough now for me to see that Maretta wore only a shirt and the woman wore nothing at all except her wig. Tony got no chance to say anything. It must have been a shock anyway, being dragged into the cold like that, away from the warmth of such a body.

Two men held him by the arms and two men hit him, with fists like rocks, deep in the kidneys. Then they swung him round and hit him again, in the stomach, and he went down like a dead man.

During this time the four other men had seized Kim by the arms and legs and lifted her from the ground. Her body writhed and twisted in their grasp but she made no sound, nor could she. A thick band of black tape had been fastened across her mouth, making it look like a wide gash where the tongue had been torn from its roots.

She writhed again, her limbs pale silver in the early light, and the absence of any noise at all made her movements seem like some slow and ghostly dance witnessed from a long way off.

But this cruelty wasn't sufficient and someone grasped her wig and ripped it from her head and all that was left was her pitifully short hair, hardly growing as far as the ears. The four men lifted her up now and threw her, face down, across the bonnet of our car and there they held her and she gave up the struggle, knowing there was nothing more she could do under the power of those rough hands, with her legs spread-eagled and her arms held down.

Now they dragged Tony to his feet but he could hardly stand and so they held him upright. One of the men drew a knife and slit the shirt down Tony's back, pulled it off his arms and threw it to the ground. Another slapped him around the head a couple of times to make him look, propelling him closer to the woman. I kept motionless behind my tree trunk, twenty yards away, and did nothing but stare.

The man with the knife leant over Kim and drew the blade along her back and across her buttocks once or twice. Again she tried to move but couldn't. They were going to cut her up, and I knew they were, but still I did nothing.

At that moment a light flickered in the windscreen of the other car and one of the eight men went to it and reached out a phone. The message, whatever it was, was short but effective. Kim was released and left lying across the limousine and Tony was dragged to the grass and thrown down there. The men got into their car, reversed it out of its slot and drove away just as quickly and silently as they had come. It was over.

Kim was the first to move, pushing her body up from the car with her arms and tearing the tape from her face. Then she got her clothes from the limousine's rear seat and dressed. When that was done she looked around for her wig, found it and put it on. And all this time Tony lay where he was, rocking his body to nurse the pain.

But at last Kim got him to his feet and draped a beach robe from his shoulders, and with their arms around each other, they walked slowly towards the pavilion behind me, their path bringing them within a yard or two of my tree, but as they went by I moved behind the trunk and remained invisible to them. They said not a word and the woman was not even weeping. Soon they were gone and in a moment I heard a door close.

I was sober now, quite sober, and I stepped out from the shelter of the dark. The sky was taking on colour and I could hear the animals beginning to move in the undergrowth. The air had lost its chill and the ornamental lake was shedding its hard surface of grey.

What I had witnessed might never have happened, only I knew it had because the door of the limousine stood open and Tony's shirt still lay on the ground in two pieces. I went over and threw both halves into the car and walked away.

Back in my room I wanted a drink badly but felt too sick for it. My hands were trembling. Why had I watched and not done a thing? Why had I not shouted or screamed or crept away to telephone the police? Was it solely because I might have been seen and beaten up myself? I winced at the very thought of it. I could never take a beating; even the threat of it would have me grovelling.

But that wasn't the only reason; it was not even the main reason. I knew why I had done nothing. If the Mexicans thought Tony Maretta had the money, it wasn't likely that they would think I had it, and that idea was a great consolation to me. Yet this consolation did not live long. If the Mexicans were sure their man was Tony Maretta, why on earth had they left him in the middle of their work, and what had the telephone message told them?

This was a question that made me jumpy all over again but I knew I couldn't answer it and there was no point in trying. I pulled off my clothes, swallowed a tranquilizer and half a bottle of mineral water and rolled into bed. Somehow I had to get a couple of hours' sleep before they woke me for breakfast and another day's work.

8

The Man Who Knew Too Much

The telephone jangled like a cow-bell and a bright female voice wished me good morning, reminding me that I was still the recipient of hospitality at the Treetops Hotel. I replaced the receiver in its cradle and stared at the ceiling in despair. On awakening I had enjoyed a micro-second of blessed innocence but the succeeding moment had annihilated it and now everything came back to me in a rush: my hangover in the shape of a sickening headache and my fear in a clear picture of the cruel dance I had seen just a few hours previously.

I swung my feet out of bed and waited for the room to settle. Then, when I was ready, I heaved myself upright and edged my way gently into the bathroom. Once there I dropped an Alka-Seltzer into a glass of cold water, drank it and got into a fierce shower, not getting out of it again until I felt nearly human. What, I wondered, would this new day bring?

The day itself brought very little and the events I had witnessed the night before might have been nothing but the remnants of a dream. On my way to the restaurant I went by the limousine and looked inside. It was as clean as if it had just been delivered by the hire company. Maretta's shirt was not where I had thrown it and there were no traces of Kim's belongings either—no coat, no handbag. I looked at the car where Kim's body had been held—there wasn't a smudge on the polish. I studied the grass where Tony had fallen—nothing. And at breakfast neither Tony nor the woman were visible.

"He's got a lot to do," said Alex. "We'll see him later."

The others were like they always were in the mornings. Dull, waiting for their blood to warm: everyone living quietly inside their own skulls with no wish to come out until noon.

While the others lingered over their coffees I loaded the gear into the station-wagon. Then I sat in it with the doors open, watching the squirrels like a man who had never seen such things before. Nothing looked real to me that morning; nothing felt real, not the clear light of day nor the remembrance of the things I'd seen.

What should I tell Ernie and the rest? Anything at all? Or should I wait and see what Tony Maretta said? I could talk to Angela, of course. She was the only one who was likely to take what I said seriously, but what could I say to her? That I had watched two people being humiliated and had done nothing to assist them, too spineless and too selfish even to shout or to run for help. Would I be able to admit to such cowardice when I knew that to do so would take more courage than I had ever possessed? I clicked my teeth; I had better camouflage myself in silence, that silence that was the first and best resort of people like me.

So I worked hard that day and watched my companions through every minute of it, though I noticed nothing out of the ordinary. As our hangovers diminished, the normal back-chat of a film unit at work took over and eventually everyone, except me, began to relax.

We had hired a cocktail bar somewhere in Santa

Monica, within sight of the ocean, and we spent the whole day there doing interiors of Deegan in a series of situations that were meant to show the attractions of the Espionage range. We had also hired three local electricians, half a dozen extras, male and female, a props man and a make-up girl. We were quite a crowd.

It was fortunate for me, I suppose, that during the day the strange, unreal world of the film we were shooting became real, and the outside, real world of Los Angeles, never terribly real to me anyway, began to distance itself. The dangers that threatened me, actual or imagined, seemed to fade in the artificial light of our lamps until finally they disappeared altogether. Even at lunch-time this illusion of safety continued when we went to a so-called "English pub" and were served "real" ale and sausages and mash by girls with accents that had been born in Glasgow and Manchester.

Once or twice, while we were working, I made half-hearted attempts to talk to Angela, but both she and I were kept too busy; she was always searching for props or running errands for Ronnie and I was always changing lenses or re-loading magazines. Eventually I gave up thinking altogether, something that is not difficult for me, and pushed every single one of my anxieties from my mind.

But that was not an answer. My own little dream factory could not protect me for ever and before long the shooting came to an end and I was once again sitting in the back of our station-wagon, staring at the streets as they went by, and only too aware that my illusion of well-being was progressively and speedily disappearing as we neared the hotel. The Mexicans were in the streets, and in the

Church of God's Will the Reverend was waiting and I was
going nowhere until he was satisfied.

The phone rang while I was in the shower and when I
answered it I heard Ronnie's voice telling me that we were
all to meet in Tony's room just before dinner. As I followed the path through the trees from my pavilion to his I
fell in with Ernie.

"It's nothing much," he said, "something about them
Mexicans who gave us the going over at Newport. Seems
they turned up again last night, but I didn't see them. Did
you?"

I answered automatically, as always protecting myself
against involvement. "No," I said, "I left the disco early,
with Nick—at least I think I did."

Tony looked well and I couldn't see a mark on him. He
was neatly dressed in white trousers and scarlet shirt and
was sporting a chunky gold bracelet on his left wrist. Alex
was already there, so were Nick and Ronnie, and just as
Ernie and I went in through the door Angela appeared on
the little terrace beyond the window.

Tony handed us a drink. "I don't want to exaggerate the
importance of this," he began, "but I had a little trouble
with those guys from Newport. They roughed me up a bit
this time . . . and Kim as well."

"Is she all right?" asked Ernie, and Tony smiled, con-
struing this interest as merely lecherous.

"She's fine. She's gone down to San Diego, she's got
friends there."

"What did the police make of it?"

"They can't make much of it at all . . . same as before.
They think we've got mixed up in some gang squabble."

"How could they mistake us for someone when we don't
even live here?" Nick looked puzzled.

"If we knew," answered Alex, "then we'd go and tell them, wouldn't we?"

"What makes me think the police are right," continued Tony, "is that when these guys were roughing me up there was a phone message through to their limo and they just went away . . . didn't even tell me what they were after. It looks to me that someone has at last told them they were barking up the wrong tree."

"That was lucky," I said.

"It was," said Tony, but he didn't look at me to say it. "What I really want to emphasise is this. First I don't want any of you to worry about what's happened. The police think it's all over now . . . these guys will have discovered their mistake and will leave us alone. Second, and perhaps more important, I don't want Deegan worried by what I've told you . . . so just don't talk about it when he's around. We've only got four or five more days of shooting left and I want it all to end on a happy note. If this Espionage thing works out well there'll be plenty more where it came from . . . and we could all do with that. Okay?"

At this we all nodded sagely. We were accustomed to producers telling us that there would be more work in the future if we behaved ourselves. But my thoughts ranged elsewhere. I had been intrigued to notice how little Tony had told us about the beating he had received. He had not described the viciousness of the attack, nor the cynical cruelty that had been shown to Kim.

It was, as he had said, possible that his only reason for being discreet was to avoid alarming Deegan and, through him, those that managed him. On the other hand, if Tony did have the Reverend's diamonds there could be other reasons. He would be hoping, for example, that whoever controlled the Mexicans had called them off for good. That would leave him in the clear—then all he had to do was keep his head down for a while and pick up the diamonds just as soon as it was safe. On that day he would be ten million dollars the richer and could begin shooting his own feature film if he so wished. Fine for him, of course, but not for me. If the heat was off Tony Maretta then on whom would it fall next? As I saw it there was only one answer to that question and I didn't like it. The heat would be on me.

Once we'd finished our drinks and the meeting had come to an end we drifted out onto the verandah and from there set out, across the grass, in the direction of the restaurant. I lagged behind a little and waited for Angela, who was bringing up the rear on her own.

"Do you think I ought to tell the police about the diamonds?" I asked her. "I mean that's why the Mexicans beat Tony up, I'm sure of it. I think the cops ought to know. I think I ought to tell them about the Reverend as well, shouldn't I?"

Angela stopped and faced me. She was taller than I was. "I don't think the Reverend would appreciate you discussing his business with the Los Angeles Police Force," she said.

"He might get angry?"

"He might get angry. In this town it's okay to shout your mouth off about yourself, get a little publicity, but in matters like this, Del, it pays to do as you're told and keep your head in the trenches, otherwise you might get it shot off. Just do like I do. Do your daily stint and nothing more. Listen and that's it. And my advice to you is the same."

"But I'm sure Tony has them, I'm sure. Why doesn't the Reverend go after him?"

"How the hell should I know. I'm a farm girl from Iowa. For all I know, and in spite of what you say, you could have them yourself."

"Don't say it!" I could feel myself going pale. "If the Mexicans got even a whisper of that I'd be as dead as a kipper."

Angela nodded, not at all reassuringly. "Then do as I say. You'll be flying out of here in a few days."

"The Reverend says I'm not going anywhere until he has his diamonds."

"That's tough," said Angela, "but if you're telling the truth you're okay. If you're not then that's something else, really something else."

We went on and crossed the car park outside the restaurant. There I noticed Ronnie talking to a couple of men who were leaning, arms folded, against a police car. Once again I slowed my pace and allowed Angela to go into the bar ahead of me. Then I began to retrace my steps in the direction of pavilion seven, as if I had forgotten something. I had made up my mind. Notwithstanding Angela's advice, I simply had to tell someone what I knew.

I walked slowly past the police car and as I did Ronnie laughed with the two men, said goodbye and went into the hotel. I spun on my heel immediately.

"You are police officers?"

"Uh-huh," said one of the men. He was broad across the shoulders and heavy across the stomach. He wore a gun on his belt and behind him, inside the car, a pump-action shot-gun was clipped to the dash. "I'm Lieutenant Hackenbowne." He unfolded his arms and looked down at me.

"I saw the incident last night," I said, "or rather early

this morning." My speech stumbled and I could hear myself being unconvincing. "It was pretty nasty. They stripped the woman right off. I'm sure they were going to rape her but then this call came . . . to the car."

Hackenbowne folded his arms again and crossed his ankles. He looked comfortable against the warmth of the car. He nodded and said nothing. My voice dried and he waited awhile before speaking.

"Yes," he said. "Could you recognise any of these men?"

"No," I said, "I was too far away."

"We've had a full statement, believe me," said Hackenbowne. "I don't think there's anything you can add to it."

I didn't like Hackenbowne. He was big and strong, black-haired and red-faced. He'd seen it all: murder, rape, mutilation, addiction and extortion. A little, forty-year-old camera-assistant with a prim voice, imported from England, did not impress him at all. He spoke again, saturated with boredom.

"But anyhow we got no descriptions worth a shit and the woman's left town and don't wish to prefer charges. I gotta shrewd idea that there ain't a lot we can do. And if we find 'em, you can bet there'll be a hundred mothers who will swear blind that these boys were home all night playing cards and drinking."

I took a deep breath. "I think they are looking for some diamonds, and they think we've got them . . . ten million dollars' worth." As I spoke I knew it was a mistake. Even in my own ears it sounded hysterical.

Hackenbowne folded his arms the other way and glanced at his companion from underneath dark brows.

"Ten million dollars. How come?"

"I went to the Church of God's Will and a man called the Reverend told me he'd lost that much. He was convinced that one of us knew about it . . . that's why the Mexicans are interested in us. There was a man killed in London, just before we left . . ."

"A man killed in London!" Hackenbowne shook his head in ironic disbelief. "You don't say."

At this Hackenbowne's colleague grinned and walked round the front of the car and opened the door on the far side. He slid behind the driving wheel and switched on the engine. Hackenbowne stood up straight and smiled. "You're a privileged man," he said. "I never met anyone yet who got to see the Reverend in person. I never have, though I know some of my men worship at his church. . . ." Hackenbowne let the sentence hang fire for a second or two. "He does an awful lot of good works. . . . He has a hospital for junkies, and a village out in the hills somewhere. Diamonds, you say. I'll certainly look into that. I'd hate for the Reverend to lose anything . . . anything at all."

I swallowed hard and half-raised a hand like a little old lady trying to hail a cab. "I was telling you this in confidence. You know, just in case it could be of any use."

Hackenbowne nodded understandingly. "Sure," he said, "don't worry. I won't tell a soul. And thanks." With this he opened the door behind him and ducked into his seat. The car reversed and with a squeal of over-soft tyres it bounced across the ramps and went down the drive to the highway.

I watched it go and swore to myself, many times. Angela had been right. I should have kept quiet—now I had spoken out of turn and God alone knew what might come of it.

9

On the Waterfront

"I phoned her this morning before work," said Nick, "but she wasn't in, so I left a message with her flat-mate."

"Who?" I said. We had spent another eight hours filming in Santa Monica and on our return Nick and I had got to the bar at Treetops first.

All day I had hardly spoken, worried about having opened my mouth to Hackenbowne, but in the end the time had passed without incident and I felt reassured. I had seen no Mexicans, apart from waiters and gardeners, and there had been no sign of the Reverend or his acolytes. Perhaps it was all over; perhaps the diamonds had finally arrived by some other, unexpected route. It was even possible that my talking to the police had scared everyone back into the woodwork. In Los Angeles nothing was surprising.

"The waitress," answered Nick, "the good-looking one with the waterbed."

"Oh, Waterbed. I thought she said you were too old."

"It's worth another try."

"When are you taking her out?"

"Tonight if I can get my hands on the station-wagon. She's down in Balboa, on somebody's yacht. Her flat-mate said she was coming back this afternoon."

"I wish I'd been a woman," I said. "Just imagine, sex whenever you feel like it, paradise."

"You wouldn't have wanted to have been an ugly woman, would you?"

"Of course not—a good-looking one."

"Well, you aren't a good-looking fellow, are you, particularly? What kind of good fairy is going to work this miracle for you? Turning you from an ugly bloke into a beautiful woman? She wouldn't half have her work cut out, like digging the Panama Canal."

I stared into the bar mirror and wondered, yet again, how different my life might have been had I grown into adulthood with the features of a Maretta or a Deegan. If an inch more on Cleopatra's nose would have changed the course of history, what might it not have done on the end of my penis? It didn't bear thinking about, the luck of the draw.

"Let's go out on our own tonight," I said. "Let's go down to that cinema where all the stars put their hands and feet into wet cement."

"I've already asked Tony for the car, just in case."

"Why don't you phone Waterbed at Balboa? Find out if she's coming back. If we don't leave now we'll be stuck here all evening with the others. I need a change."

"I'll phone her flat-mate for a number, okay?" He went away to the telephone and before long Angela came and sat beside me.

"Want a drink?" I asked her. "Nick's gone to the phone."

"I saw him. He's phoning that waitress, isn't he? He's wasting his time, those girls get asked out all the time."

"Fannies of gold," I said. "Wish I'd been a woman."

"I doubt it," answered Angela as her drink arrived. "You'd have to put up with men for a start."

"Do you like this town?"

"Well, the one thing that Waterlooville gives you is a sense of perspective. Yeah, I like it."

"Is that so," said Ernie. He was washed and changed and sat down on the bar stool next to us.

"Hello," said Angela, "how's Ernie?"

"Tired. The next person to mention Espionage gets castrated. . . . If it's you, I'll have to think of something else."

The barman, a Mexican I hadn't seen before, leant on the bar. His shirt was open to the waist and his brown skin was covered in curly black hair. He made Ernie's drink and added it to our on-going bill.

"Nick and I want to go out in one of the cars tonight," I said. "Maybe see that cinema."

"There's no end of places," said Angela. "What do you fancy?"

"I dunno, that's why I'm asking you."

"I saw Maretta drive off in the station-wagon," said Ernie with satisfaction. "God knows where the limo is."

"Alex has gone to get someone," said Angela. "He's bringing her here for dinner."

"Where can you go?" Ernie went on. "You'll only end up in a restaurant like this one, with a disco like this one and with a barman like this one."

"It's just to make a change, that's all. Just to make a change."

Nick came in from the telephone. "Who wants another drink?" he asked.

"Did you speak to her?"

"I got her flat-mate, there was a message."

"I thought she was on a boat."

"She is. They've all got radio phones, those million-aires."

Angela slipped from her stool and left the room.

"She won't be back until tomorrow."

"Angela?"

"No Waterbed."

"So we can go out then?"

"Yes. We'll just have to wait until Alex gets back."

I had to be satisfied with that. I put my empty glass down and as I did Ronnie entered the room and made his way over to us.

"Get you girls a drink?" he asked.

"Where's Deegan?"

"His manager flew in today . . . Barry Keeling . . . they're having a long chat. . . ." Ronnie began to sign bills on the counter and a new cluster of drinks waited for us. "What shall I get Angela?"

"Just a Coke." Angela slid back onto a bar stool. She held a lighter and a pack of Marlboros in her hand. Her face was bright now, emptied of the day's tiredness.

"You and Nick going out tonight?" asked Ronnie. "Anywhere nice?"

"I'd like to go to that cinema where they have the im-prints in cement," I said. "I'd like to say I saw a film there."

"That's a good idea," said Ronnie. "Maybe we should all go, for a change."

We remained quiet for a while. Two waiters crossed the room and I glared at them suspiciously. Suddenly Ernie leant forward and jutted his face into the middle of our group, low down, about the level we were holding our drinks.

"Look at these four men, just come in," he whispered. Slowly our heads turned, sheepish with circumspection. "Christ!"

I drew a deep breath, scared by what I saw. The four men were so big that they moved as if unused to gravity. Each swing of the foot was the swing of a millstone; their hands were as big as wheelbarrows, their limbs were slabs of granite.

"Keep your voices down," said Angela. "You don't mess around with guys like that."

"Have you seen 'em before?"

"Yeah, in every state of the Union."

The four men ignored us completely. For all our staring they hadn't bothered to notice us. The barman went towards them, smiled and then held his hands on the counter like doves. The leader of the four men said something immediately and the barman, with more affability than I'd seen during all my time at Treetops, nodded in our direction and the leader saw us then and looked.

His face, I noted, was in the same proportion as the rest of his body, so big that there seemed no way to assemble it into a unit. I studied an ear, a nostril, a mouth, a solid wave of hair and an eye, but however hard I stared I could not grasp the whole face in the breadth of my brain. It was as if I had suddenly lost the faculty of seeing in three dimensions.

The man came along the bar, levering his knuckles on top of it as he advanced. His companions loaded their hands into their pockets and stood without moving. They didn't order drinks, they didn't sit down and they didn't talk to the barman.

"Who's running this film crew?" said the man. His voice was not loud but it vibrated in such a way as to make me think my teeth were loose. He was used to getting his own way and had been for a very long time.

There was silence while we all looked at each other. Strictly speaking, Tony was in charge of the unit but he was absent. We finished looking at each other and then looked at Ronnie.

"I'm the production manager," he said. "The producer's not here."

"You're under-crewed," said the man. "I run the local branch here and you need to take on three more men, you're working light."

"Under-crewed," echoed Ronnie, and he pretended to laugh at the very idea. "That's ridiculous. We have exactly the right crew for what we are doing. We cleared it all with our union before we left England."

"To hell with your union," said the man. "That's over there and this is over here, and when you're here we tell you whether you are fully crewed or not, and you're not. That's all there is to it. You need another man on camera, at least one more on sound and a stills' photographer . . . this girl's non-union."

"A stills' photographer," said Ronnie, and raised his eyebrows and twitched his neck. He was glowing warm in spite of the air-conditioning and I felt sorry for him. "My producer won't wear it. We can't afford it."

"Then your producer can't afford to film here," said the man. "You won't shoot another foot in this state, or any other state. You can pack your bags and go home."

"What are you talking about?" It was Alex. He had joined us without attracting our attention. The woman he had brought with him stood a yard or two away from us, along the bar.

"He says we're under-crewed," said Ronnie. "He's a union official."

"A union official," said Alex. "How do we know that?"

The man's hand went inside his jacket and brought out a card, showed it and then put it away.

"You're wasting our time," said Alex. "We've got a full British crew, our union has passed us okay and that's all that matters to us." Alex was showing off in front of the woman, but he was also being very brave.

"You the producer?"

"The director."

"Well, I'll tell you what I said before you got here. I'm the union branch as far as you are concerned and you are under-crewed. For the rest of your time here you take three of our men, one on camera, one on sound and one on stills . . . I'm trying to do this nice. I could make you pay these guys for all the time you've been here already."

"A stills' photographer," Alex was shouting now, "you must be crazy. If you don't get out of here I'll call the police."

I looked towards Angela but she had moved to face the bar and was holding her head in her hands, staring into her drink.

The man shook his head. "The police! What's wrong with you guys? I'm trying to do this thing nice because you're from England and maybe don't understand the way we work around here."

"I won't discuss it any more," said Alex, sounding very British. "Just go away."

It was then that the man stopped being polite, grasping the front of Alex's jacket and gently folding it up in his massive hand. "You must be flying or something. What are you on, cocaine? I'll tell you one last time. There will be three members of my union out here tomorrow and they'll be working with you guys. However long you stay here, you pay them. They know the rates. If you don't, you don't get to finish your film. There'll be no processing and your gear falls into the sea."

"Threaten as much as you like," retorted Alex. His coat was tightly bunched up now and although he flapped his arms he could do nothing. None of us made any attempt to release him.

The man shook his head again, his amazement genuine. He released Alex and watched him smooth the creases out of his coat. As he watched, his face became more serious, as if he'd only been playing before.

"Okay," he began with a sigh, "just once more I'll tell you. If you don't do as I say you are going to get yourself cemented into a freeway . . . do you understand that? No film, no equipment, no crew, no director."

There was a silence until Angela spoke into it. I'd been waiting for her to. "I think you'd better do as the man says." She didn't turn from her position at the bar. Her head was still in her hands.

Alex was angry, very angry. He was unable to do anything and we weren't going to help. His body shook. He glanced at us and then, out of frustration, for he had no chance of hurting him, he pushed the man in the chest and walked away.

The man didn't like that and lifted his hand to grab Alex, but Ronnie, overcome by an unseasonable rush of altruism, clutched at the man's arm and wrenched at it. "Steady on," he said, "none of that."

The look of amazement came over the man's face once more. He seized Ronnie in one hand, shook him as if he were all that was left of a skinned rabbit and then swatted him twice across the head, hard. When he had finished he dropped Ronnie to the carpet and moved away, pushing us all to the side with one careless sweep of his arm.

There was another silence, dreadful this time, smelling of shock and fear. Alex stood motionless by the side of the woman he had brought. Angela sat by the bar, resolutely not showing her face, and the rest of us waited, standing in a semi-circle. The four union officials strolled from the room and we watched Ronnie curl up on the floor in a tiny ball of pain and shame.

As the men went through the door, Angela moved, kneeling by Ronnie's side and dabbing his forehead with iced water from a jug, using her handkerchief. We crouched beside her. Ronnie's face looked like an empty house.

"Is anything broken?"

Ronnie's right eye was swelling; so was the left one. The skin was badly bruised; his nose was bleeding.

"Jesus," said Ernie, "should we call a doctor?"

We helped Ronnie to his feet and perched him on a bar stool.

"Oh God," he said, "where's my drink?"

"Get him a brandy, someone."

I examined the group of people around me. Every one had been purged of apathy. We were all angry, all excited, all a-buzz with blood.

Alex turned to Angela. "The bastards," he said, "what do I do?"

"You do like the man said," she answered. "You've only got three or four days to go. It won't cost you so much. He's right, you're lucky he didn't make you pay for the previous ten days also."

The telephone on the counter rang and the barman rose

from behind the bar where he'd been crouching and answered it. He spoke once or twice and then handed the receiver to Nick.

"We mustn't let it get us down," said Ronnie bravely, "and we mustn't alarm Deegan. Remember . . . this was just union trouble." He tried to smile even though Angela was holding a wet cloth over his face. "Let's all have a drink."

"That's it," said Alex, and he put his arm round the new woman. "We'll have champagne . . . Hey, barman! Let's have three bottles of champagne, and we'd better have a raw steak for my friend's eye."

"Sure thing," answered the Mexican, "you got it."

I was standing next to Ernie and was surprised to see that his face was flushed. He looked unstable, like gelignite ticking down to some appointed explosion.

"You know," he whispered so that only I could hear him. "You know, there comes a time once or twice in your life when you wish you could really believe in the power of prayer, real power, when you want to pray like Samson prayed. Just one moment when you wish you were young again and stronger than anyone else on earth, strong enough to pull down the whole bloody temple. Just so you could get hold of that union man and snap his spine over your knee. I'd give a lot for that, a lot."

"Yes," I said. "I suppose it would be nice to be Superman. Imagine going straight through the wall, flying with your fists in front of you and zapping the four of them, one after the other. Splat! Pow! Zunk! It's no good though, Ernie. Shrimps is shrimps. Ducking and diving is my family motto. It's carved on the escutcheon."

Nick put the phone down and came back round the bar. "It's that bloody Waterbed. It was her again. She's not coming back tomorrow either now. She's staying on that bloody boat."

"That's great, we can go out."

Alex shouted down the bar. "We'll have a special dinner tonight. In Ronnie's honour. Champagne all the way."

"Yes," said Angela, and she took the steak from the plate the barman had given her and held it against Ronnie's eye.

Alex came down the bar and handed me the car keys. "Here you are," he said, "'f you want them." The bundle slid into my hands.

"Hey!" said Ernie, "you can't leave us tonight. We've got to stick by Ronnie, haven't we?"

"What about it?" I said. Nick was staring into the counter, looking puzzled. "I said what about going out tonight?"

"Oh . . . I don't know. I don't really fancy it now. Anyway, I suppose we ought to eat with the others, really, after what's happened."

I pushed the keys back along the bar to Alex. "You'd better keep them. Nick and I will probably go out tomorrow night."

"Yes," said Nick, "that's a good idea, we could always go out then. It will be better tomorrow."

"That's right," agreed Ronnie, "we could all go."

10

Way Out West

In spite of the champagne dinner we started work pretty early the next morning and completed what was left of the cocktail bar scenes before lunch. Afterwards, taking Angela along with them, Alex and Tony decided to look at some locations down on Venice Beach.

"You can have what's left of the afternoon," they said, "and we'll see you back at the ranch tonight."

The moment I got into my room at Treetops I canned up the rushes and sent them off by messenger to be processed. That accomplished I took a shower and wandered through the trees once again, looking for Ernie in the reception area.

"Why don't you try the golf club," said the receptionist when we asked her to suggest a place that wasn't so gloomy as our usual bar. She had a sun-dug face yet in the cold air-conditioned air she warmed herself at an electric blow-heater.

"You should wear more clothes," I said.

The receptionist rubbed the goose-pimples on her forearms. "They make it so cold in here, they're crazy."

"They certainly are," said Ernie.

Outside I let the sun warm my skin. We were standing on a patio and not far from us was a corner of the palm-fringed lake. All around us the scenery was neat and disciplined and a row of silent Mexicans, like characters in a nursery rhyme, swept pine needles from the brick-trimmed paths. Ducks and drakes watched us from the undergrowth.

We set off along a path that dipped behind the restaurant and followed the edge of the water. Here we saw more ducks and they quacked for bread we did not have. We strolled on, crossing a rustic bridge built in branches of concrete that had been painted brown to make them look real. Rabbits hopped out of our way.

"They're all waiting to be discovered by Walt Disney," said Ernie.

"What did you think of that union business?" I asked, and Ernie shrugged as he walked.

"Like I said to Ronnie," he answered, "Tony thought he could get away with it and he couldn't. You can't, out here. Angela had it right. That union guy let us off lightly. It could have cost a whole lot more."

"Those three men they sent today didn't do a thing. They just sat outside in their car and read the sports section."

"Well, there was nothing for them to do. They seemed nice enough."

We crossed the tennis courts and now the ground swelled up in soft mounds of sculptured green. Here and there bright pennants showed where one or two of the holes were. A stand of dark trees leant against an enamel sky that had been baked the frailest of pale blues. I trod on a golf ball and stooped to pick it up. "Ace Quality" I read in gothic print.

"A friend of mine trains his dog to find these up on Wimbledon Common. He makes a fortune reselling them." I bounced the golf ball once on the path and put it in my pocket. "I'll take it home for the kids. I've got six already."

A four-wheeled caddy-buggy grew out of the top of the nearest mound, bore down the slope and zipped electrically past us. It carried two old men and two young men with golf clubs, baseball hats and Bermuda shorts. They floated steadily onwards, sitting rigid, in the direction of the tennis courts.

"They come out to get exercise and then drive everywhere," said Ernie.

"Perhaps it's for the fresh air."

Ernie laughed in a way that was no laugh at all. "Fresh air in Los Angeles, you're joking. You should have seen what I coughed up this morning, looked like lentil soup."

We arrived at the clubhouse and climbed some steps to a porch. Here we found a few chairs and tables, made from bamboo, but they were all empty. Everyone was inside, in the cold. We went on round the verandah, pushed at an entrance and went into the bar. Four men sat in a corner playing cards. Two or three others were perched on stools talking to the barman, who was polishing glasses the way they do in the movies.

"He's waiting for Walt Disney too," said Ernie. "Two beers."

"You Australian?" asked the barman.

"Only when I'm drunk," I said.

Ernie paid for the beers and I picked them up and carried them through the door. I didn't want to freeze inside.

We sat and sipped. "Ah," I said. The four men who had passed us in the buggy were now out of it and searching for their ball more or less where I'd picked it up. I took it out of my pocket and put it on the table.

"You've ruined their day," said Ernie as if it were the best thing I'd done since leaving England.

"How's Ronnie?"

"Okay. He's taking it easy by the pool. Lovely pair of black eyes."

"He's a nice guy . . . he was only trying to stop trouble."

We fell silent. It was enough to sit in the sun. There was a flip, flip, flip from a water jet as it twitched in circles. The caddy-buggies hummed this way and that, quartering the landscape. Every now and then large, middle-aged Trojan women in short pleated skirts strode across the verandah, their studded boots rippling on the concrete and their wide thighs looking mottled and damp, like corned beef fresh from the tin.

I finished my frozen beer. "This stuff's awful."

Ernie finished his and stood. "Want another?"

"Yeah, might as well, they don't do any harm."

When Ernie had gone I stretched out my legs and looked at the nearest bit of skyline. As I did, yet another caddy-buggy began to appear, rising slowly from out of the ground, just as if it were living at the end of a long focus lens. Others rose up behind it in the same deliberate way. I didn't like this and I was right not to like it. My spirits sank. I had been off the hook too long. I could see several of the caddy-buggies now, a little fleet of five, diminutive and seemingly harmless, but their passengers were not golfers, they were big men trying to look at ease in tiny transport. They sat forward and upright, dressed in their well-fitting suits of dark blue. The Reverend himself wore a fawn suit, a fawn shirt and a dark brown tie.

Silently the fleet came to a halt and the Reverend stepped to the ground and moved easily up the steps to the verandah. He moved with the same grace I'd noticed before; a large man, he was full of an immense physical power that was made to appear all the more powerful in being so easily restrained by the irresistible sinews of his mind. He was like one of those eternal images from the dream factory: he possessed star quality in abundance and he wore it like a cloak.

Then the acolytes stepped down too and stretched their limbs. Three of them climbed the steps also and went to stand by the entrance to the bar, their hands demurely folded in front of them. The remainder stood in small groups and talked, but all the time they kept watch across the golf course, their eyes wary. The Reverend lowered himself into the chair next to mine, leant forward and laced the fingers of one hand with the fingers of the other.

"It is good to see you again," he said. "I was told that your filming will be over in three or four days. I thought I'd come to see how you were . . . and what you have to say."

For two and a half days I had been enjoying a relaxed normality. I had pushed my last meeting with the Reverend to the back of my mind, and in the artificial light of the cocktail bar at Santa Monica and in the heat of hard work, I had forgotten about the Mexicans and the man opposite me. The business with the union officials had been unpleasant but it had pushed me to the side-lines, a place where I naturally belonged. Now that comfort fell from me and I felt exposed once more. I swallowed and remembered what Angela had said: "Tell the truth and behave normally." After all, the Reverend was a man of religion; he had to believe me in the end.

"We've been working very hard for the last few days," I said, "and then we had trouble with some union officials."

Ernie had been gone about ten minutes and I was missing him. I twisted in my chair and at that moment he came through the door. He had a glass in each hand and a rare smile of sociability on his face. I wondered about that smile until I saw that he was followed. Ernie had made friends at the bar and had brought his prize back with him. The Reverend's acolytes looked a question at their master but he only smiled and Ernie and his new chum approached the table.

"Hi," said the man, raising both hands to shoulder level, "howya-doin'?"

"Sit down, Bob," said Ernie. He looked at the Reverend, half-recognising him. "Didn't we meet the other day?"

The Reverend nodded and smiled. "I have come to talk to your friend about the work of my church. I think he is destined to help us. I hope you don't mind?"

"Not at all," said Ernie, looking cheerful. "Del could do with some Christian counselling. I'm talking to Bob here."

Bob sat next to Ernie on the far side of the table and grinned all over his body. "Nice to see you," he said, and I watched him extinguish the light in that part of his mind labelled "sincerity." "Name's Bob Laverbee, Artisan Film Productions, from up Thousand Oaks way." He hooked a proud thumb at his chest. "Producer."

The Reverend stared at Laverbee, took him all in—thin arms, knobbly wrists, short-cut silver hair, mean face, narrow skull—and threw him out again. Then he turned to me, and Ernie and Laverbee were on their own.

"The union men are where they are for your protection," he said. He lowered his voice though it was still the same one as before—warm and moist with tentacles. "It was done like that because I don't want anyone to connect those men with me for the time being. Their lives would be at risk."

"Protection?"

"Yes, I did not like the incident the other night when your producer was beaten. But there is more to it than that. I am obliged to protect my interest, you understand, in this case you . . . As I mentioned once before, because they wish to do me harm those who have hired the Mexicans would kill anyone they suspect of knowing where the diamonds might be, more especially if they thought that person was not telling them everything he knew; and even if it meant the diamonds were lost forever."

Laverbee beamed around the table. He could obviously hold a warm smile for hours and must have developed special muscles for it. "I'm a writer too," I heard him explain to Ernie, "more of a writer than a producer really . . . but then you have to turn your hand to everything in the film business." He wriggled on his chair as if preparing his anus for inspection. "What kinda budget you got? If you'll excuse me for askin'."

"It's a big one," said Ernie, and I saw the dollar signs come up on Laverbee's pupils.

I looked back at the Reverend. His stone gaze had not left me. "I really don't know what this is about," I said, speaking in my sincerest voice. "I'm just a camera-assistant out here on location. That's all I am. What you see you get."

The Reverend leant back in his chair. "I am not un-civilised," he said, "but I am determined to have my way. I am not a violent man either, yet I will do anything for the sake of my Church. If you can prove to me that you are not involved, then I will of course look elsewhere, but all my information—and there is a lot of it—points to you.

Nevertheless I will suspend judgement for a day or two; it suits me to do so. That much time you may still have. Afterwards we shall have to talk seriously. You see, in the Church we are poised to make a great move forward and my enemies know this. They know too that once I have possession of this money that great move forward will be made and I shall be unassailable."

"Yes, but they could kill me by mistake."

"They never do anything by mistake. In any event they will be quiet for a few days. I have them off balance. They were told that I had already received the diamonds by way of another courier. Your producer and his lady were lucky. The message arrived just at the right moment for them."

"From you?"

"That is why those men left. Once I have those diamonds they will have other priorities, like staying alive."

"You mean you'd kill them?"

"They are taking advantage of my preoccupation in another area. In a little while I shall not be preoccupied."

"That's why it's been quiet?"

"Yes, but it won't last much longer. They will soon discover that I have been playing with them."

"The old days are gone," said Laverbee to Ernie on the other side of the table. "They are not interested in a real story any more, a real talent. Twenty-five versions of *Rocky* as long as it will show a profit."

"I phoned my wife the other day," I said. "My house had been broken into and two strange men were asking questions about me."

"I know," said the Reverend. "I have sent some of my men to London to deal with them."

"Hassan Sabor," I said, but I did not say it aloud.

"I mean," said Laverbee, "they're more interested in

getting people to go sight-seeing round that studio than making films in it."

"Perhaps the Mexicans have the diamonds already. Maybe that's why they've gone quiet."

The Reverend shook his head. "I do not think so," he answered. "I have a source of information amongst them. They were convinced your producer had the diamonds . . . and that was because the person who really has the diamonds laid a false trail."

My throat tightened.

"You were overheard talking to the girl at the swimming-pool. Later you drank too much and said something to a waiter. When the Mexicans reappear they will be angry, and angry people do violent things. I may not be able to protect you all the time, either from them or the necessities of my own situation. Very soon my little hospital may be the only safe place for you."

Ernie and Laverbee continued their conversation. The water jets turned and flipped and I felt like shrieking with fear but somehow managed not to. The Reverend's followers waited patiently and the sound of a golf ball being struck came clearly across the grassy mounds.

Ernie stood up and collected the glasses, leaning across the table. "I'm going to get some more beers," he said.

The Reverend didn't even bother to look at him but Laverbee nodded his head, so did I, and Ernie walked away.

"He's such a nice fella," said Laverbee, raising his voice. "Known him long?"

"A good few years."

Laverbee shook his head in wonder, as if my friendship with Ernie were too bright and beautiful to contemplate even. "I came to meet someone for lunch," he continued, leering confidentially as if to imply that meeting people for lunch was an acceptable sexual deviation that men could brag about amongst themselves.

Ernie returned with the beers and set one down before me. Laverbee shifted round to face Ernie as he sat and went on with their conversation.

"This is the story of a fine man with a past spent outside the law, who goes to pieces when his wife dies. He is brought back to reality when, some years later, and because of his drinking, a boy is killed during the robbery of a big silver shipment. Then this broken man returns to the Indian tribe that had saved his life once and raised him . . . there he becomes the man he was before. Then with an Indian companion who is also an enemy—a nice irony there—he sets out on the long trail of revenge and redemption and rediscovers the country he once loved—the West —the West that was to become America."

"My Church," said the Reverend, "works in the world to make it a better place full of better people, and nothing is allowed to come between us and that goal. I do not wish to harm you, or indeed anyone, but my Church is worth a thousand like you. My Church will do good with this money . . . my enemies will do nothing but evil."

"And do you think I could sell it to those assholes at Universal? I couldn't even give it to them. 'The Western is dead,' they kept saying. I tell you it's that damn Cimino and his *Heaven's Gate* movie, he's killed the Western for another twenty years. Forty million dollars it cost. What's the use?" Laverbee opened his palms to the sky as if he expected a signed contract to drop into each.

The Reverend leant towards me so that he could speak quietly. "I have much to do, and time is short."

"This missing money," I asked, "where did it all come from in the first place?"

"Donations, followed by wise investment which at the same time advanced the cause of the Church. Money, often the instrument of the devil, has been doing God's work instead."

"So I'll have to produce it myself," said Laverbee, "and I'm nearly there. I have most of the capital already. I've got off-shore money, mad money and oil money. All I need now is a quarter of a million to put up the insurance bonds. I've got my director lined up, and my star . . . No, I can't tell you that. You know this business—it's impossible to keep a secret in Hollywood, it's a village."

The Reverend looked at his three men by the door and they moved towards him. Then he glanced back at me—a glance of absolution. "I don't want you to worry," he said. "There will be a day or two of quiet yet. Since our last meeting we have been praying and the future has become clearer. I appreciate that God is working through you in some mysterious way. I appreciate your coolness too, believe me I admire it, but it is to me you will have to come in the end. I am the man and there is no other in this city."

With these words the Reverend rose and walked away, taking his magic with him, and I felt diminished the moment he had gone. I crouched in my chair and watched his fleet of buggies retreat over the crest of the nearest rise.

The Reverend had aroused all my sleeping fears. Contrary to his vision of the near future, I would not have the diamonds when he expected them and I would not be able to hand them over to him. I began to think about what would happen then and a picture of the junkie lying on the floor in the Church hospital formed in my mind. That might well be me in a few weeks' time.

"I don't really want to get involved in that Turkish money," said Laverbee, "though the scenery's great out there. If I have my way I'll shoot it in Arizona, where it happened."

"Is that a non-union state?" asked Ernie. "We've had some trouble over here with the union."

"I can shoot in Arizona, no problem."

"Two hundred and fifty thousand dollars," said Ernie wistfully, as if it were just a question of running down to the bank. "How soon can I see a script?"

The door off the verandah opened and the barman stood there, handsome, smiling. "Telephone, Mr. Laverbee."

Laverbee sprang to his feet and smiled all over his body again. "I gotta-run-along-now," he said. "It's been great, Ernie. I'll drop the script into reception." He slipped a card out of a pocket. "There's my number. Call any time you're not shooting and we'll make a night of it. Okay?" Suddenly he stiffened his arm across the table and aimed his hand at me like a bayonet on the end of a rifle and I shook it. Then, with one more brief flash of that smile that seemed to live on its own somewhere, Bob Laverbee waved and walked into the bar.

"Ernie," I said, "this religious guy here, this Reverend, he thinks I've got what those Mexicans were looking for, down at Newport. Diamonds, Ernie, diamonds. I'm scared. I want to get out of here."

Ernie shook his head in a superficial gesture of sympathy. "I know," he said, "the whole place is crazy but I think my guy was crazier than your guy. I just happened to say that we were out here making a movie and he took me for a big-time producer. He wants me to invest a quarter of a million dollars in some Western of his called *Seth Hanna*. This whole town is mad. I'll be glad to get on the airplane myself, believe you me."

11

A Touch of Evil

As soon as Angela got back from Venice Beach that evening, I took her back to my room and poured her a drink. We sat on the little terrace and watched the shadows of the trees lengthen.

"The Reverend came to see me today, over at the golf club. He still thinks I have these diamonds, and those union men . . . he said they were to protect me from the Mexicans."

"He's very thorough, the Reverend," said Angela, "very thorough."

"That's as may be but if I need protecting then I don't want to be here to be protected. I want to get on a plane and go home."

"Got any money?"

"Not much. I won't get paid until I get back to England. I've got my air ticket and a credit card."

"You wouldn't get out through L.A. International, you'd be spotted for sure. You'd have to get away from the hotel without being seen and hop a bus to San Francisco, fly out from there. That might work . . . but Del, if the Reverend believes you have what he wants then there's nowhere for you to run."

"And the Mexicans. If they find out that the Reverend

thinks I'm the man then I'll be in real trouble. What can I do?"

Angela held my hand. "All you can do is like I say. Lie low. Those diamonds may turn up all on their own. You've got a couple of days, you say? Keep calm, go on with the job, don't talk about it to anyone and I'll try to figure a way to get you out of town. Don't let them get you on the run."

It was easy for Angela to say such things but on the run was precisely where I wanted to be. That night, in spite of her advice, I thought seriously about leaving. I even got as far as packing a bag. But it takes courage to run away. It takes grit to leave the comfort of the hotel room, stepping beyond the windows and the terrace, walking towards the unlit golf course.

On the other side of the nearest trees lay the dark land of the republic, stretching under the sky for three thousand miles—a wild country, still peopled by savage tribes waiting in ambush. So instead of leaving, I sat in my armchair and drank too much. Frightened into immobility and indecision I stayed where I was, slept fitfully, rose the next morning and went, after breakfast, tame and apprehensive, to Venice Beach with the others.

"Orson Welles," said Alex as we drove along, "shot a film on Venice Beach."

I was riding in the limo. Alex and Tony sat in front; Ronnie, the bruises on his face less livid now, was beside me. Deegan had gone in Angela's car and the others were in the station-wagon. It was just the way it had worked out.

"He was acting in Westerns then and they called Charlton Heston. Universal it was. 'Heston,' they said, 'how'd you like to be in a movie with Orson Welles?'

" 'I'll act in anything Orson directs,' he said.

" 'Directs!' they said, 'Hell!' So they rang Orson again and said, 'Hey, Orson, how'd you like to direct Heston in this film? Only it's got to be for the same money.'

" 'Sure,' says Orson, 'just send me the script and I'll re-write it for you.' So he does. That's the way to make mov-ies. It won an award in Brussels and ran two years in Paris and yet the studio hated it."

Tony, who was driving, came off the Hollywood Free-way and onto Highland Avenue. Behind us came the sta-tion-wagon and behind that the three union men in their own car.

"Are we paying for their transport?" I asked.

"Yes," said Tony, "and their meals."

"It was a good film," said Ronnie. "I saw it on TV. It had Marlene Dietrich and Joseph Calleia, remember him? He was in *The Glass Key.*"

"Never heard of him," said Tony, "or the film."

"Shame," said Alex, and he stared out the window at the empty pavements. "Venice was a wild place then, full of winos."

"It's still crazy now," said Tony. "Painters, poets, drop-outs, junkies . . . and all the tourists come to watch . . . all coasting and steaming along, each in his own sweet way."

"What is this Venice Beach?"

"It's where people go. They say there's a murder a day in Venice."

"That's nice," I said. "What time?"

Tony Maretta stopped the car and we got out into the morning sun. I stood for a moment bewildered by bright colours and the presence of thousands of people. It was as if the abandoned boulevards of America had sent their ghosts here to walk and play. The street in which we had parked was full of clarity and sound, violence and strength.

A black woman, taller than any of us, bowled by on roller-skates. She braked, spun in a circle, hands on hips and looked us over. She was dressed in a leather tunic and tights, nothing else. She spun in another circle and glided into the crowd.

"What are we shooting?"

"I don't know," said Ernie. "Just grabs. Deegan is searching for someone, we never know who. It's part of a montage sequence. Atmos, bits and pieces."

I nodded and went to the back of the station-wagon and got out the gear. The three union men walked over from their car and watched me work. "Hi," I said. I didn't mind them watching; they made me feel safe. They seemed more human than the Reverend's acolytes, less monolithic.

The cameraman was called Benny Webb; he hadn't touched a camera, ours or his, since he had joined us. Then there was Joe Lavin—a stills man who hadn't taken a still—and last of all a small-boned, so-called sound-engineer who didn't carry a recorder. He was older than his companions with a face as full of cracks as an oil-painting. When he spoke, his saliva rasped against his teeth as if he had a mouthful of tin-tacks. His name was Ermal Thruman and he looked as friendly as a roll of barbed wire. In spite of the Californian sun he always wore a jacket and trousers of heavy tweed, and the jacket always bulged and swung with the weight of something that might have been a pistol.

Ernie came over and looked at the four of us. "Just bring a few spare mags," he said, "and a spare battery. Leave the tripod."

We walked to the corner in a group and the road that ran parallel to the shore opened up on our right and left, noisier and more crowded than the road we were leaving. The ocean was near us now but the beach was invisible beneath brown bodies and bright parasols. The sun was hard and hot. Lines of houses, brick built and pretty, faced the sea. At intervals, and opposite to them, along the edge of the beach were benches and small pavilions. In front of me two young women sat, embracing, holding back the noise and creating a calmness within the circle of their arms. They kissed.

I hurried on in the wake of Ernie and the others. He had the camera on his shoulder now and I carried a holdall with the spare magazines in it and a battery on a belt. I also carried the lens box and the clapper-board. When I caught up with the others, Ermal caught up with me.

"Let's all stay close," he said, and he took the clapper-board. "I'll take this. You look like a Christmas-tree."

We walked southwards. Above us, at the windows and from the balconies people pointed and laughed. The road was lined with stalls and Deegan stopped at them all, talking to people, asking questions and peering into the crowd. The undercover agent, pursuing his enemy into dangerous and unknown territory.

And it was. The sun burnt down and perspiration crept into my eyes and made them smart. I blinked, and tried to take in everything at once: cyclists, skaters and joggers. On the café terraces people sat and talked. Drunks stumbled and stared at us as we walked by, and those on other drugs sat in quiet corners and gazed inwards, examining what they saw there.

A small mob of the curious followed us everywhere, and this crowd—white, black, Chinese, Mexican, African and Arab—made the three union men nervous. This was not a place they were used to or liked and they looked as if they were waiting for something to happen or for someone to arrive. Every now and then Ermal shook his head as he handed me the clapper-board.

"It makes me jumpy down here," he said. "It's full of lunatics—Cubans and wets. You never know what they will do. And junkies . . . all flying on something. They ought to round 'em all up and send every last one to the gas-chamber."

But the others were not aware of this tension. They were enjoying themselves and so we went on shooting: body-builders, dancers, face-painters, fortune-tellers and a man who lived in a cardboard box and sang songs for money. For three hours it went on until the enjoyment went and we became short-tempered and tired, then we stopped at last because there was no more film. Back at the car I stowed the gear away and Joe and Benny smiled with relief and Ermal gave me the clapper-board.

"It sure is a crazy place," he said, as if he had reached this judgement after a lifetime of deliberation. "You know, sometimes it's hard for me to realize that this is my own country down here." His voice sounded sad, as if he was ashamed of Venice Beach and was trying to apologise for it.

I slammed the tail-gate and we crossed the road and joined the others by the beach and we sat together on a low wall and ate the hamburgers and drank the beers that

Ronnie had ordered up for us. The crowd still promenaded past but we were part of it now, our work done and the camera put away.

As we sat like this, we heard a light metallic chiming coming from close by and suddenly, out of the throng, a young man sprang before us, carrying a guitar and dressed in green, like a jester with golden shoes that curled upwards at the toe. His jacket was slim at the waist and decorated with silver thread. It was stiff too with hundreds of tiny bells sown upon it.

"Hey, you guys," he yelled, "I been looking all over. Don't you move now before you've heard old Jingles speak."

"Aw shit," said Ermal. "Another damn looney."

"I ain't so looney," said Jingles. "In fact I ain't so looney at all. This is as far west as you can go, brother; any further and you drown."

"Thanks a million," said Ermal, and drank from his can of beer.

Jingles approached the wall, crouched and looked at us all in turn. "Did you know," he said at length, "that the tribes are back? Did you know that? You thought you'd buried all them damn Injuns but someone has dug them up. Yessir. The Pawnee, the Wahpekute, the Shoshone, the Ogala, the Arapaho, the Chippewa and even the Apache from over the border, yessir! They're back. Circle the wagons and send for Liver-Eatin' Johnson." Jingles struck a chord on his guitar and shook his body so his bells rang. I looked at the others and they were all smiling—all, that is, except Ermal and his two friends.

"Johnson," continued Jingles, "was a mountain man and whenever he killed himself an Injun, which was plenty, he sliced him up with his trapper's knife, cut out the liver and ate it while it was still warm. He declared that it was the finest eating delicacy on God's earth. 'Prime meat,' he said. He couldn't let no Injun walk by him but out would come that hunting knife and zip! Out would come that liver too, steaming hot and wet, the blood dark and rich. Johnson got so fly at taking them livers that an Injun could walk on maybe ten miles before he even realized his liver was gone . . . Yessir."

Jingles ended his story here and rose to his feet, striking his guitar again and producing a discord. As he did the big black woman on roller-skates came down the road at speed, leaning forward and pumping her legs, weaving through the crowd but touching no one. She made straight for Jingles, swooped like a big crow, spun to a halt, shouted something I didn't understand, and then went as rapidly as she had come.

Jingles struck his discord again, shook his body to make the bells ring and jumped forward so fiercely that he frightened me. But he only crouched once more, this time at Ermal's feet and looked up into his face. I saw his bulging eyes, the sweat running down his neck.

"Time to get back to the fort," he said. "Crazy Horse has left the reservation." And with that Jingles jumped into the air, turned his back and ran off into the crowd.

The three union men threw down their beer cans and stood, not hurrying but not taking their time either. Benny looked at Tony and Ermal looked at me: "We're going back to the hotel," he said. "Do any of you boys want a ride?"

"I'll come," I said. "I'll come back with you."

In the car I stared from the back window and watched Venice disappear. "What was that about?" I asked. "Who was that Jingles?"

"I don't know for sure," said Ermal. "Sells junk for the

Reverend, I guess. Anyhow, he was telling us that trouble is coming . . . so we left."

"They made a film about that Liver-Eatin' Johnson," said Benny, "with Robert Redford. They prettied it all up though, didn't even show him eatin' Injun livers raw. Damn shame."

"There was another thing," said Joe. "Did you notice? That Angela, the girl from Iowa. She wasn't with us back there. She's disappeared."

12

This Happy Breed

We arrived back at the hotel well before the others, and Ermal booked a room in the same pavilion as mine while Benny and Joe moved into the one opposite.

"It'll save us time in the mornings," Ermal said, and he smiled. "I gotta toothbrush in the car."

"Do you think Angie is all right?" I asked. "I mean, why would she disappear like that? Is that what Jingles was trying to tell us?"

Ermal looked over my shoulder at his companions. "Hell," he said, "who knows? We don't know this Angie. She could be anybody. Don't worry. Remember she lives down there in Venice. She probably ran into some boyfriend and they went to bed for the afternoon. She'll be back by breakfast, you'll see."

But Angela was not back by breakfast and as soon as Tony came into the restaurant I asked him. "Did she disappear yesterday? Are you keeping it quiet so as not to upset Deegan? It's them Mexicans again, isn't it?"

Tony sat and poured himself some orange juice. Waves of his body rub came over the tablecloth at me. "Don't be melodramatic, Del," he said. "Angie phoned through last night. She ran into some people she knew and went to a party at some guy's house. That's all."

"When is she coming back?"

"She was having a good time, so I told her to come back tomorrow, or later. It's the way they live round here, Del, moving on all the time. This is Venice Beach, not Barnes."

"Mortlake," I said, wishing I could think of witty answers for people like Tony. "It's Mortlake I live."

I thought the day was going to be awful after a start like that but it turned out fine. In fact it was the most agreeable day of the whole location. It was Deegan's last so Tony was determined that we should have fun.

We started early and drove up to Santa Barbara, and when we arrived we found an endless beach where the locals set up stalls to sell the things they made: souvenirs like pottery, bracelets, jewellery and paintings. That day I thought of my two kids and bought them a railway locomotive each, all hand-carved out of wood.

We didn't do much in the way of work and no one seemed to mind. We shot a few sequences in the market and that was that. As soon as it was lunchtime Ronnie booked us into a restaurant with a terrace under palm trees and we took our time eating and enjoyed it.

I thought we would do some more shooting that afternoon but Deegan and Tony talked for a while and decided that we had more than enough footage of the Espionage character. All that remained for us in the next couple of days was some pick-up shots which we could do on our own, without Deegan. That afternoon we were for the beach.

So we got into our bathing trunks and dozed for a while and watched the women swimming and coming out of the water, looking naked in their wet, tan-coloured swim-suits. I stretched my limbs and felt good. Everything was so bright and blue I felt proud, as if I possessed the afternoon, endless, like a child's afternoon. Somehow I had slipped into that perfect postcard where the glamorous and the great live.

I fell asleep at some point, and when I awoke, Deegan was sorting through a pile of drift-wood he'd gathered. Most of the pieces were long and twisty, made grey and sapless by the sun and salt. He knelt and selected three straightish lengths and pushed them into the firm sand by the edge of the ocean so that they stood upright.

"We haven't got a bat," I said.

"Yes we have." Deegan held up a wedge-shaped piece of timber, its sides rounded by a hundred thousand waves. "And I even nicked a tennis ball from the hotel this morning."

"You are not going to play cricket?" said Ernie.

Alex jumped to his feet, scooping up the tennis ball. "Certainly we are," he said. "It's the only game. Just think what a country America might have become if they'd only learnt to play cricket."

The three union men rolled over at this and gazed at Alex with empty eyes. Benny and Joe had swum but even now, sitting on the beach, Ermal was still dressed in his jacket and trousers.

"Oh yeah," he said.

"Oh yeah," said Alex.

"It's Deeg's last day," said Nick, rising from his towel. He flexed his arms and shoulders with a bowler's motion. He liked any sport, anything that made him move his body and helped him to feel it moving. "We'll all play, one against all."

Tony pointed at the union men. "Those buggers can play. Come on, Ermal. It's just like baseball."

"Yeah," said Deegan. "There'll be champagne for the winners, and for the losers too."

"I was good at baseball," said Ermal suddenly. "I'll show you guys."

"You go in first, Deeg, show 'em how it's done."

"One over for practice," said Alex, and he walked away, measuring his run. We spread into fielding positions, shouting at the three Americans, telling them where to stand, what to do.

Deegan tapped the sand with his wedge of driftwood and I moved from one side of the pitch to the other, searching for a spot where the ball was least likely to go. Alex turned and ran gracefully up to the bowler's crease. The ball was a good one. Deegan missed it completely and Tony took it behind the stumps.

"What the hell was that?" shouted Benny. "Why does he pitch like that? He looks like a ballerina."

"You're not allowed to throw in cricket," said Nick. "You have to keep your arm straight."

"We played on the River Kwai," chanted Deegan, waving his bat over his head, "even though we were dying like flies we managed one last over, one last boundary. Up and down the Burma Road there were wickets chalked on every brick wall."

We had spectators now. About fifty of them, and the number grew all the time. They observed us seriously, their eyes following the ball wherever it went, listening to our chatter.

Deegan was bowled, then Tony took a turn, then the rest of us. At last the union men came forward, grinning and looking sheepish. They played well, their eyes trained by a childhood full of baseball. Even Ermal enjoyed himself, removing his jacket and giving it to Benny to hold.

"I'm gonna lick you limeys at yer own game," he cried, and the large crowd clapped their hands at every stroke he made, and when he was out at last, he beamed into the applause and made the deepest of bows.

"It's the only wisdom the English brought with them to the earth," explained Deegan, "how to spend a lifetime playing games and the intervals in between taking tea . . ." Deegan broke off here and waved and shouted to someone beyond the crowd.

I turned, as did the others, and there was Ronnie, absent during the match, a rapturous grin bursting through the bruises on his face. He, too, shouted at someone behind him and the crowd fell back to make a path, and two waiters from the restaurant where we'd lunched came into view over the slight rise in the sand, carrying a trestle table. Behind them was another waiter bearing a stack of folding canvas chairs, and behind him three more men with cold boxes, ice-buckets, napkins and fruit.

The crowd closed in again. Their voices rose and they laughed. We laughed too and looked at Deegan while the table was planted in the middle of the wicket and its legs pushed into the sand to make it secure. Once it was, we placed the chairs all around and the cool boxes were opened and bottles of champagne were laid out. There were cakes as well and biscuits and more fruit. Then, when the waiters had finished, they stepped back for a second, gazed at their work, smiled and went away, flitting across the beach.

It was a happy moment and once again I felt I had slipped into that postcard world of primary colours: the exciting world of Espionage after-shave. This was real and everything else was insane—Los Angeles, the Reverend, his Church and even the God that lived in it.

"Some guy, that Deegan," said Benny.

"He ordered it when we were at lunch," said Ronnie, "and I arranged it all."

"A toast," said Deegan, "a toast." He raised a dripping, frosted glass. The Pacific Ocean behind his arm was crashing onto the shore. "Here's to a great location, a great crew, a great cricket match."

Solemnly we held our glasses aloft. "Here's to you, Deeg."

"Good luck with old Espionage."

The crowd thinned. Others passed by or came to stare for a second at the odd sight of the table and the wicket, but they did not stay long.

Steadily the sun crossed the sky and soon it was time for us to leave, time for Deegan to catch his plane.

"Come on guys, one last drink at Treetops."

We got up from the table and gathered our belongings. Deegan pulled on a sweater. "Drunkenness stopped play," he said.

And so we walked up the beach, our feet dragging through the loose sand, leaving the table stark and lonely, with the wind whipping at the white cloth, leaving the sky and the foam-tipped waves behind us.

"I ain't had such a day since I was a kid," said Ermal.

Pulling away from Santa Barbara I felt a boundless and over-powering melancholy growing within me. I had wanted that day's contentment to go on for ever; now it was gone and I was going back to another world, one that had always despised me and wanted to do me harm. When would the Reverend claim his due? I shivered and clutched once or twice with my toes at the sand running loose in my socks.

"Ah," said Benny, as we drove along the Pacific Coast

Highway, "if only life was like that all the time, wouldn't it be grand?"

"Yeah," I said, "it would, but how the hell do we fix it? Tell me that! How the hell do we fix it?"

Deegan stood amongst a jumble of dark leather suitcases in the reception area at Treetops. His manager stood beside him. Gradually, as we said our goodbyes the porters took the suitcases and put them into the limo.

Deegan was going to Honolulu for a week's holiday before flying home. He was dressed in a white suit, a shirt of pale green cotton and highly tooled Texan boots. His hair had been shampooed and lay on his skull, ordered and obedient; his Californian tan was even. Deegan was a star again, travelling down the galaxy at the speed of light, away from me. I stood amongst the group, awkward, watching him turn into a stranger. He flashed his white teeth the way he did in close-ups.

"Well, thanks," he said, "for everything."

"Goodbye, Deeg, see you at the rushes."

Then they got into the car and Tony drove it away.

There was no disco in the bar that night and so, before heading off to my bedroom, I had a couple of quiet drinks with Nick. We were both feeling sorry for ourselves. Me, for all the usual reasons, and Nick because he hadn't nailed Waterbed yet and the end of the location was looming. Then she strutted into the bar and sat on the stool next to him. It was her day off.

"I been out to Torrance, see my kid," she explained. She cuddled her large breasts and placed her elbows on the bar.

"You have a kid?"

Waterbed looked round. "There's no music here tonight. I forgot. I can't live without music. Yeah. I gotta kid. I ain't gotta husband though. He used ter beat me up and all that good stuff. Wadja-dooderday?"

"We played cricket on the beach."

"What did you do?" asked Nick.

"Well, I went to see the kid. Then I visited a few places. You see I'm a dancer. I bin in a lotta stuff. Modelling too. You have to go places where the people in the business go. Phoned my agent. I get to do a lot of auditions also. Hell, some of those guys make you strip just for the fun of it."

"You like living in Los Angeles?"

"Sure. I've been a lot of other places but this is the best place in the world. Everyone says so. Who wants to live in Cabbageville? Yeah, I like the space I'm in."

"How about coming to a night-club?" asked Nick, his voice devoid of any real hope.

Waterbed was quiet for a while and looked into the bottom of her glass. "Naw," she said, "I'm too tired. Tell you what though, as you're leaving in a couple of days, why don't you come back to my room and we'll have a drink there, just to celebrate you going to Europe. You can talk to me while I'm having a bath." She smiled like weed-killer over Nick's shoulder and included me out of her invitation. "But no funny business. Nothing physical."

Together they left the bar. "You pour your waterbed, you lie on it," I called after them, but they didn't hear me.

I finished my drink and looked around. The bar was almost empty and no one was watching me—no one that I could see anyway. I said goodnight to the barman and set off for my bedroom, following the access road because, although no short cut, it was lit by big yellow lights, while the path that went between the bushes and the trees was dark and forbidding.

The Reverend had said it wouldn't be long before the Mexicans came out into the open again. I tried to remember how long it had been since I'd seen him at the golf club. Was it a day or was it two?

I kept to the middle of the road, walking on my toes, glancing to right and left. I stepped carefully into the shadows at the entrance to the pavilion. I halted, still on my toes. I pressed myself against the wall like they do in spy movies. I listened hard but I heard nothing except my own breathing.

Quietly I slipped my key into the lock and opened the door as slowly as I could. In the small hallway to my room I listened again. Nothing . . . or was it nothing? Wasn't that someone's breathing I could hear above my own? My heart began to race. I tried to calm myself. After all, I only had to cry out. Ermal was upstairs and Benny and Joe were opposite. I slid my feet over the carpet. I touched the light switch and the central lamp came on.

The room was empty. I looked into the bathroom; that was empty too. I let my breath fall out of my mouth and closed the door behind me and the noise of it woke the person sleeping in my bed.

She sat up and twisted her body round to look at me. It was Angela with bruises on her face to match Ronnie's. Her lips were swollen where she'd been beaten. Her hair was filthy and she'd been crying. A gasp of fear rose in my throat but wouldn't come out. If Angela had been to a party on Venice Beach it must have been some Donnybrook and I didn't want an invitation. I put my hand to my forehead and it felt damp. Was this the end to a perfect day?

13

Two for the Seesaw

It wasn't quite.

I advanced into the room.

"What happened to you?"

Angela let herself fall back against the pillows. "I went off to buy a Coke," she said, "and the next thing I knew I was surrounded by these Mexican guys. They dragged me into a car and took me off someplace. I don't know where. Some broken-down quarter, near a chemical works. I don't know."

"But you phoned to say you were at a party."

"Sure I did. They were gonna carve my face up if I didn't . . . and a lot more besides. You don't mess around with those guys . . . if you do you don't mess around for long."

"Would you like me to call a doctor?"

Angela moved her head. "No, I just keep bathing my face in cold water. Here." She fumbled in the bed clothes and threw me a flannel. "Wrap some ice in that."

I went to the fridge and pulled out the ice-tray. At the same time I pulled out the gin bottle and some tonics and poured two big ones.

Angela held the ice-pack on her face with one hand and

raised her glass to her mouth with the other. I sat beside her on the bed.

"The more I see of this place the more scared I get," I whispered. "What did they do to you?"

"They knocked me around a little. Stripped me, made out they were going to fool around with my body. Just generally broke me up into little pieces. Listened to me talk, then they pumped something into me with a syringe and then we talked some more." She showed me her arm.

"Heroin," I said, "that's what the Reverend does. He turns you into an addict."

Angela smiled as well as she could with her swollen lips.

"He told me," I insisted. "Showed me his so-called hospital."

"The Reverend is a good man," said Angela. "I'm sure of it. He just believes in fighting evil as strongly as evil fights good. Nothing wrong with that. It's what the world needs."

"Why did they take you? Why not me, say, or Alex or Tony?"

Angela sat up in the bed, swopped the ice from one side of her face to the other and took a deep swig of the gin. "I guess," she said, "because they thought I was still part of the Church and they wanted to know what the Reverend was thinking."

"Part of the Church," I said, "you?"

"When I came from Iowa, first off, I couldn't get any work. I was on the floor, no money, no confidence, no friends. Then someone told me about these encounter groups and I started going to them. I met the Reverend . . . you've seen him . . . he's no ordinary man. At the time it was just what I needed. I moved out to the Reverend's village in the hills and everything was suddenly different. I was a brand new person."

"Then you left?"

"Yeah. I appreciated what the Church had done for me but I wanted to see how far I could get without help."

"The Reverend, did he like that?"

"The Reverend doesn't stop you. There's nothing to say you can't go back."

"And what about these Mexicans?"

"They wanted to know about the money . . . the diamonds. They thought I might know who has them."

"But you didn't."

"But I didn't."

"Who are these Mexicans anyway?"

"They're somebody's catspaw. They are just in it because someone who doesn't like the Reverend, and what he does, has hired them in."

"But who are they? Do you know?"

"I'm not sure anyone knows . . . people who don't like the way the Reverend fights evil, I guess."

I reached to the floor and picked up the gin bottle and refilled our glasses. "Why do you think this money is so important?"

Angela laughed. "Money is always important, Del. All I know is that the Reverend wants to found branches of his Church all over. He wants to make the whole country a better place. For that he needs money."

"Well, if he's so holy why are there these people willing to do anything to stop him?"

"How the hell should I know? What I do know is that they are the enemies of a fine church. They don't like what the Reverend is doing—he's too tough for them—so they hire in a gang of Mexicans to do their dirty work."

"And that Mexican hanging from the Hollywood sign the other day," I said, "whose dirty work was that?"

"I dunno," said Angela, "but they deserved it. It's the only language they understand. Look what they did to me. Beat me up. Would've raped me for the hell of it. Pour another drink. You English don't understand a thing about the States."

I went to the fridge for some fresh tonics, poured the drinks and sat down again. It was true; I would never understand America. I took a big gulp of gin by way of compensation.

"All this money I'm supposed to have hidden away, where does it come from?"

"From the encounter groups, I suppose; you have to pay for those. And then there's rent in the village, taxes; you give a certain amount of your income to the Church, but wherever it comes from it is all spent doing good, the Reverend sees to that."

"Why'd you come here anyway? To my room I mean?"

"I came to warn you, Del."

"Warn me, oh Christ!"

She laid a hand on my arm. "Don't blame me, Del. They had me tied down, you know. They came at me with a needle. What would you have done?"

"I'd've talked," I said, "talked like I was never going to stop."

"I didn't tell them much but it was all they wanted. When they heard that the Reverend was sure it was you that had the money, they lost interest in me. They don't like the Reverend but they know he doesn't make mistakes. As soon as I came round they threw me out and I came here to tell you. You're next on their list, Del. I'm sorry."

I buried my head in the coverlet and Angela's hand stroked my hair. I waited for a moment or two and then, when I could speak, I said, "How many times do I have to say it? I haven't got a thing."

"Are you telling the truth, Del?"

"Angie, can't you see what a coward I am? Do you think I'd go through this for money—a million, two million? Courage is not part of my make-up. Isn't that obvious?" I raised my eyes and looked at her. She stared deep into my eyes. "I'll be a snivelling wreck," I said. "Even if they cut me to pieces all they'll get is blood."

I slumped to a sitting position on the floor and emptied my glass into my mouth. I wanted to sleep. "I've got to run," I said. "I've got to run and you've got to help me, you've got to tell me the best way to get out of here."

"Don't try it, Del," Angela said. "It'll make things worse."

"Worse! How worse? I'm going whether you help me or not."

Angela thought for a minute. "I'll get the times of the buses tomorrow," she said. "As soon as it's dark you call me. No luggage. Get down through the park to the highway without being seen. I'll have a taxi waiting and it'll take you to the bus station. Don't get out of the cab until you see me. Then you go to San Francisco and you catch your plane to London from there. Okay?"

"Anything that gets me out of here. Why can't we go now?"

"You're drunk," she said, "and so am I. I'm gonna take a bath."

She was right, of course. The gin had taken its effect and I was not very good at standing up. I even fell over my trousers as I tried to pull them from my legs. Angela must have heard the noise I was making because she re-appeared, dripping wet from her bath, dragged my clothes off and rolled me into the sheets.

My brain was out on its own now and the wall opposite me was rising and the ceiling was swooping and diving towards it. Just before I became unconscious I was aware of Angela's warm body, smelling of soap and eau-de-cologne, as she slipped into the bed beside me.

To begin with she cradled my head on one of her shoulders but I didn't like that and moved my head down until it was resting somewhere softer. She didn't seem to mind and I suppose we lay like that the whole night, cuddled up all lonely and helpless like the babes in the wood, except I hadn't dropped any pebbles to show me which was the safest way out of the forest.

14

The Great Escape

Ernie came in through the door the next morning walking just a yard behind the Mexican boy who brought the early morning tea. He saw the shape in the bed beside me, took a look at the head of hair on the pillow and went right out again, not saying a word.

I got up and took a shower and when I came back into the room Angela was dressed. She put a cup into my hands and poured herself a second.

"I'm going now," she said. "And don't say anything about me being here. Your friends will only get the wrong idea. I won't be coming back either. I'm gonna take a little time off in Waterlooville. I'll call Tony later."

"What about tonight?" I asked. "In fact, what about right now?"

"Not before tonight," she said. "Look, don't worry. They won't try anything as long as you stick close to the crew. Just don't wander off like I did. You got those three guys watching out for you, remember."

Then she put her cup down and went, only pausing at the door to kiss me lightly on the mouth. "Call my number just as soon as it gets dark," she said, "and I'll tell you what to do."

I walked to the restaurant, once more staying out of the

parkland, and wondered how Angela knew that the union men were there for my protection. I couldn't answer my own question. Maybe they had told her; maybe I had, in my cups. Perhaps it didn't matter.

I went up to the breakfast bar and took a bowl of corn flakes and ordered sausages and then crossed the room to sit at our table. Ernie, Nick and Tony were already there. As I sat down they all looked at me and grinned. Ernie must have told them about the girl in my bed.

"You're a dark horse," said Ernie. "Who the hell was that?"

I smirked and poured some coffee. "Some girl I met in the bar last night. Nick went off with Waterbed and then this girl came and sat next to me."

Tony shook his head as if he couldn't believe I was capable of attracting any woman, let alone something of the standard that frequented the Treetops Hotel. "Any good?" he asked.

"Wonderful," I said, enjoying my triumph and forgetting that it was a fantasy. "Aren't American women the best?"

Nick nodded and buttered a piece of toast.

"Well," I said, "what about you and Waterbed?"

"It was very dirty," he said, "very, very dirty."

We carried on eating then, quietly. Ernie picked up a section of his Los Angeles *Times* from the floor and began to read. I poured more coffee and gazed through the wide plate glass window. There was a palm-fringed patio just outside and the small parking lot where cars were left when their owners registered at reception. The union men must have parked their car there overnight and now a Mexican gardener was washing it down, singing in Spanish. The sun slanted into the restaurant and the still shadow of a tree dappled our tablecloth. Everything looked bright and clean and joyful.

Alex and Ronnie came from behind me and sat with us. Alex called a waiter and ordered bacon, tomatoes and hominy grits and pancakes.

"It'll just be Gee-Vees today," he said. "Beverly Hills, those big houses, cars going by, some of the sights, nothing much . . . and then that's it. We can all go home."

"I'm going to fly down to New Orleans," said Nick. "Just for a week. Do you want to come, Del? Share a room?"

I shook my head. "I just want to go home."

"I might go to San Francisco," said Ronnie. "I've always wanted to go there. What about it, Alex?"

Alex clicked his teeth. "Tony and I have got some people to see up in Canada. A feature for next year, it's too good to miss."

Outside the Mexican had finished washing the car and Ermal was sitting in the driver's seat with the door wide open. Benny and Joe were talking to him: Joe leaning on the door, Benny sitting on the wing. I raised my hand and Ermal saw me, smiled, and waved back. It was then, while I was still watching, that it happened and it all seemed to happen very slowly, so slowly that I felt no shock—not then at any rate.

First I couldn't see through the window any more. It suddenly and noiselessly frosted over, like a broken windscreen. Then this frosted expanse became spattered with fat gobbets of red blood, which hit the glass with a noise like heavy raindrops hitting soft mud. Immediately afterwards came the low, rich sound of an explosion and the weakened window fell inwards and downwards, like a heavy curtain, and once more I could see beyond.

The car had been blown onto its side, the bonnet had gone and the windows too. A trickle of smoke rose from inside it, but then, with the rapid sound of a sail filling with wind, a ball of flame burst up like a malignant flower and the heat reached us in the restaurant where we still sat at the table, napkins on our laps. Of the three union men there was no sign, not unless that one pathetic bundle over by the trees was all that was left of a human body.

Except for the crackle of the flames there was silence for a while; then a waitress screamed and we all rose slowly to our feet and stared at each other.

The fire did not burn for long. Some people from the kitchens ran out with extinguishers and filled the wrecked car with foam. By the time that was done the police began to arrive and soon there were scores of them all over and they taped off the patio and did all the things that television movies do—they took photographs, made phone calls, sent for the ambulances and stood around and talked.

For us the day was over. We were told to wait in the bar area until we were called for questioning. On no account were we permitted to leave the hotel or its grounds.

We sat near each other in armchairs, only speaking occasionally and in little bursts. Even Tony looked pale under his tan. "Thank God Deegan wasn't still here," he said once or twice. "Thank God he didn't see it."

After an hour or so Hackenbowne came to see us and one by one we sat in a booth with him and talked. I imagined the others couldn't, or didn't, tell him much. "Yes, the union men had been foisted on us by their officials, but once we'd got used to them they seemed like nice people and we'd got on well together. No, we didn't resent their presence. Union troubles weren't dealt with this way in England."

Since the moment of the explosion I had hardly moved, nor had I said more than a word or two. The others took it for a symptom of shock, but it was more than that. I was petrified. I felt sure that the three men had been put out of the way because they had been protecting me. Now I was all out on my own with no one to turn to.

What could I tell Ernie, for example, or any of the others? Who would believe me? Diamonds! Three guys killed on my account, a small-fry camera-assistant who'd been rowed in at the last minute and had nothing to do with anything. There was only one thing going for me. Hackenbowne hadn't believed me before; now this had happened he might.

As soon as I found myself sitting opposite him, I opened my mouth and began to tell the tale. After a sentence or two he stopped me, holding up his hand and assuming a look of boredom.

"No theories," he said. "I went straight to the Reverend the other day and told him your story. He's a very nice man, he only laughed at me a little. I felt that big." Hackenbowne held a thumb and an index finger about half an inch apart. " 'I wish I had some diamonds,' he said. 'I could use 'em for the hospital.' "

"There are diamonds," I said, "I'm sure, although I haven't seen them. It's mad, I know, but no one will listen."

"I would like to listen," said Hackenbowne, "believe me, but you don't even know where they are or who has them. Have you been threatened, and if so do you have a witness? Are you a big man with real-estate that someone else wants? The Reverend says he doesn't even know who you are. Says he might have met you by chance over here, but he meets a lot of people."

I looked down at the table.

"Okay," said Hackenbowne, trying to be gentle. "Did you hear these union men talk about anything that made you think they were in danger?"

"They were nervy down on Venice Beach," I said.

A slight smile crossed Hackenbowne's weary face. "I'm nervy down on Venice Beach," he said. "So is everyone."

"Can I have your number," I said, "so I can call you if I do get some proof?" That was a lie. I really wanted the number in case the fear in me became unbearable.

Hackenbowne fished in a pocket and handed me a card. "You can call me from England. I'm getting you boys on a plane just as fast as I can." With that he got to his feet and I followed him over to where the rest of the crew waited by the bar. "Okay," he said, "you can all go, but no further than your rooms. I might wanna talk to you again."

"What's it all about?" asked Ronnie, looking at no one in particular.

Hackenbowne pulled at an ear lobe. "I don't know whether what happened today had anything to do with what happened at Newport, or the beating the other night. It still looks to me like you've wandered into some union shoot-out. Perhaps whoever it is really does think you are someone else, or even working for some company they don't like. I don't know and I'll probably never know, but whatever it is the sooner I get you out of town the better I'll like it. When do you finish shooting?"

"We would have finished today," said Tony. "Now we'll have to do the shots tomorrow and fly out the next morning."

"You do that and I'll be a happy man."

I tugged at Hackenbowne's sleeve. "Do you think we're in any danger?" I asked, "I mean from the people who did this?"

Hackenbowne raised his eyebrows. "I'm gonna round up every suspect I can think of who works in this line of business," he said. "I'm also gonna leave some men here, just to keep an eye on things . . . and as for you"—he smiled across at me, not unkindly—"I'll see there's a man outside your door all night. Will that make you happy?"

The others laughed at me but I didn't mind. "Ecstatic," I said, "positively ecstatic."

I went back to my room and locked myself in. There were lots of things I would rather have done but none seemed feasible just then. I got a bottle of gin out of the fridge, the empty one had been replaced, but I put it away again. I was still weak from the previous evening and I felt sad for Ermal and the other two. I didn't even know if they had children or wives. Bang! Just like that. Nothing left but blood all over the window.

It wasn't long before I succumbed to the idea of a drink, poured a big one and sat at the desk with it. What would the Reverend do now? Would he come for me soon? After all, that was in the logic of the situation and in a way I almost wished for it; at least it would be an end to uncertainty.

I opened a drawer and took out a small pile of postcards I had bought from Reception on the day of my arrival. I hadn't sent a single one yet and people get so hurt if you don't. Perhaps now would be a good time. I picked up a pen and thought about Ermal. How could I write a postcard when I'd just seen what I'd seen and was convinced it could happen to me at any minute? "Wonderful in California. Been to Santa Barbara and Disneyland. Saw three men blown up today, nice chaps, blood all over the place. Nothing dull about Los Angeles. Yours, Del."

It was no good. There would be no postcards this trip, no messages that might outlast me. I refilled my glass. All I had to do was wait for it to get dark and call Angela. It was time for me to run.

I was cold when I awoke. I had fallen asleep on top of the bed and dribbled onto my pillow. I swung my feet to the floor and wiped my mouth with the back of a hand. While I'd slept, the dusk I had desired so much had crept in from outside and invaded every corner of my room. Without switching on the light I went to the big window and looked out. The day was going and all I could see was a line of hills on the horizon and the trees standing up in cardboard silhouettes.

I showered and then dressed with particular care, taking my warmest and darkest clothes: a sweater and a jacket slung over my shoulders. I took all the money I had, my passport and my credit card.

I went into the hallway and locked the door behind me. Outside there was a policeman sitting on a bench. I walked up to him and said, "I'm going to the restaurant, for dinner."

The policeman raised a hand in acknowledgement and the leather of his gun holster creaked. "Best go round by the road," he said.

Outside the restaurant a great deal of work had been done. The wreck of the car was gone, the blood-stains had been scrubbed away, the potted plants had been replaced and even the window had been reglazed. Apart from the three or four policemen standing by the hotel entrance, everything was back to normal.

I was early for dinner but this formed part of my plan. I wanted the others to see me before I left. I didn't want them looking for me until the following morning—by that time I would be in San Francisco and boarding a plane for Heathrow.

It was aperitif hour in the bar but none of my colleagues was visible. I ordered a drink and took it to a table at the side of the room, near the pay-phone. I placed my drink on the table and dialled Angela's number.

"I've just got to the bar," I said. "I'll be free soon."

"Come down to the highway in an hour and a half," she said. "The driver will flash his lights twice when he sees you. I'll be waiting at the bus station. The bus to San Francisco gets there in plenty of time for the first flight to London. Okay?"

"Okay," I said, and replaced the receiver.

I left my drink and went through to the restaurant and Waterbed showed me to the table that was always reserved for our dinners. "You're the first," she said. "I ain't seen Nick yet."

I ordered some fish and a side salad and a bottle of Napa Valley white. I ate slowly and thought about how I could leave without attracting attention. There was a wide corridor leading to the kitchens. Halfway along it were the restrooms and beyond them was a large deliveries door, hardly ever closed. I would go that way. The cops outside would think I was still inside. Whoever was watching me for the Mexicans would, I hoped, not notice my disappearance until I'd been long gone. The same should hold good for the Reverend's men, whoever and wherever they were.

Ernie came and sat beside me and picked up the menu. "You're early," he said.

"I want to get to bed," I answered. "I don't feel too good . . . you know, after what happened."

Ernie jerked his head and made his face look hard. "Yes," he said. "Think I'll have a nice steak, rare." He grinned and poured himself a glass of wine. "Tony and Alex are flying out tomorrow."

"Tomorrow!"

"It seems the cops think the less of us here the better. We do the Gee-Vees and leave the next day. Ronnie's got a shot-list."

"That's great," I said, "really great. Why can't we go?"

Ernie laughed. "Don't be dramatic. I've been talking to the cops today and they say there's nothing to worry about. Tony was unlucky, he got beaten up in mistake for someone else, that's all. Nothing's happened to the rest of us. These cops know what they're talking about. They see this kind of thing all the time. That business at Newport, it was the gear they were interested in, not us . . . and the three guys who got killed this morning, well, it's all about who hires what and to whom. It's big business in Hollywood, and it's worth millions of dollars a year. You see, it'll all go quiet now, that's what the cops say."

Ernie's hors d'oeuvre arrived and he began to eat. Ronnie joined us and I could see Nick at the entrance to the restaurant, talking to Waterbed. I made no attempt to take up Ernie's conversation. I could have told him that I was next on the Mexicans' list, but as I wasn't going to be around much longer, I saved my breath.

In a little while Nick came to the table and Waterbed stood close by his chair to take his order. He held the menu with one hand, while the other was out of sight, stroking her leg. There was a smile on his face and she moved her thigh against the pressure of his fingers. I ordered and drank a coffee, looked at my watch and got to my feet.

"You going already?" asked Ronnie.

"Just a quick night-cap in the bar," I said, "then I'm going to bed."

The others said goodnight and I left. I threaded my way between the tables and walked along the corridor to the men's room. I waited in there for a minute or two, pulling the door ajar so that I could look back into the restaurant. Alex and Tony were now at their places, reading the menu, and as far as I could judge, my departure had aroused no interest anywhere.

I waited a little longer, tense and frightened, then I went quickly to the deliveries door and without a moment's hesitation, like a man parachuting from a plane, I stepped out into the dark.

The moment I was outside I turned to my left and leant against the wall to take stock of my situation. I breathed quietly and listened hard. I had never done anything like this before and the only experience I had to draw on came from my reading of thrillers and my viewing of films. I knew I had to be patient—to keep still for long periods so as not to give my position away to anyone who might be lying in ambush.

Not far from me I could see the dark mass of some undergrowth and behind it a stand of trees. There was no light where I stood except for the yellow gleam which spilled from the door beside me. After that it was all blackness.

I remained motionless for some while before proceeding,

but when I did move I did it well. I lowered my body to a crouch and flitted like a shadow across the curve of the delivery road, making straight for cover. Once there I pressed myself close to a tree trunk and yet again I waited. I heard nothing and my spirits rose. In another hour or so I would be on the bus to San Francisco, free of Los Angeles and all its madness.

Slowly, very slowly, I made my way through the hotel's parkland, creeping stealthily amongst the bushes in the direction of the highway. Every so often I stopped and listened in case I was being followed, but not a sound came to me across the night—not a sound, that was, except the distant moan of traffic on the road.

At last I arrived at the limit of the hotel's ground. I stood by a tree and glanced at my watch. I was ten minutes before the allotted time but when the allotted time came so, too, did the taxi-cab, pulling up about fifty yards from me. Almost immediately its headlights flashed twice, and keeping to the shadows still, I went towards it.

As soon as I became visible to him the driver put an arm out of his window, reached behind and opened the rear passenger door. I went closer and ducked into the car with all the speed of a rat disappearing up a drainpipe, and threw myself onto the back seat.

"The bus-station," I said, "just as quick as you like."

"Okay," came a voice over the intercom, "I know where we're going. No problem."

I stared out of the window as we left Treetops behind us. If anybody was following me it would be now that I would see their car coming out of the hotel driveway—but I saw nothing. I chuckled. Three lots of people watching for me, including the Los Angeles Police Department, and I had got away from them all.

The car gathered speed and filtered onto a freeway. It was the first Los Angeles taxi-cab I had taken a ride in and I noticed that between me and the driver was a bullet-proof glass partition, and behind it a strong wire mesh. I noticed, too, that there were no handles on my side of the doors either. That would be to stop passengers running away without paying their fares. I smiled. What a town it was where cab-drivers had to protect themselves like this. I was glad to be going home.

This feeling did not last long. For most of my time in Los Angeles I had been driven by someone else and so the labyrinth of streets and highways had left me with no clear idea of north from south, east from west. I had no idea where the bus-station was in relation to Treetops, or even if we were going towards it or not. And so, as I was driven further in that taxi, I began to grow uneasy. After all, like everyone else, I knew that American cab-drivers were loquacious to a fault, but mine had not said a word since he'd said "no problem." Then we left the freeway and all the old fears came back to me, settling round my heart as if for a long cold season.

I sat forward and peered from the window like a little old lady. We had entered what even I could recognise as one of the broken-down sections of Los Angeles. There were no lamp-posts in the streets and on either side of me all I could see were the odd shapes of wooden-built, single-storey shanties with porches that leant this way and that.

Soon the cab slowed down to little more than a walk and began to lurch in and out of pot-holes where the thin tarmac had been worn away to reveal the earth underneath.

"Where are we going?" I shouted. "This isn't the way to the bus-station."

"Take it easy," came the voice. "I know what I'm doing," and I heard what I should have heard before—the Mexican accent.

I inspected the doors again but there was no way of opening them. I clasped my hands together and I bit my lip to stop the whimpering. I hadn't fooled anyone with my escape from Treetops and I had fallen for the oldest trick in the movies when I should have foreseen it. The car sent by a friend had been replaced by one from an enemy. Now the Mexicans, or rather those who employed them, had me just where they wanted me—and the bus to San Francisco was on another planet.

15

The Big Sleep

The moment the car stopped, a door came open and I was pulled out into the warm night. I wanted to yell for help but this possibility had been anticipated and I was struck twice very hard, once in the stomach and once in the kidneys. The breath left my body in one gasp and I fell to the ground.

The pain was like nothing I'd ever known and I was paralysed by it. I thought I must suffocate and I panicked, screaming but making no sound. I was dragged upright and carried along a dirt path, up some steps and into a frame house, my feet scraping the ground all the way.

I was aware of a door slamming behind me as I was hustled along a passage and then into a large room. The light there came from one electric bulb hanging in the centre of the ceiling. It showed me three men sitting on kitchen chairs, smoking small cigars. In the middle of the room was a long table that looked like an instrument of torture with two large metal rings screwed into the top of it.

Now the rough hands that held me bent my body at the waist and my ankles were taped to the bottom of the table legs. At the same time my arms were pulled forward and my wrists were tied to the metal rings. Then someone stuck a knife into the collar of my jacket and ripped the coat and the shirt from my back. The same knife slit open the rest of my clothes and blood trickled from my skin where the blade had dug too deeply. In the two or three seconds since I had been carried into the room, I had been rendered immobile and helpless. Tied to the table I was a skinned rabbit with its arse in the air.

"Please," I whimpered, "please don't hurt me." I heard the sound of water hitting the floor and the front of my body became warm. I was peeing uncontrollably. There was a laugh and a voice said, "He's really pretty. I wanna be first."

My whole body began to tremble and I wept, big sobbing tears of abject terror. Life had frightened me before but nothing in my experience had prepared me for this. My anus felt as large and as loose as the mouth of an old sack.

"Please," I said again, "please."

One of the cigar smokers moved his chair and sat astride it, resting his arms on the back and lowering his head so that it was almost level with mine. It was Baeza, the man we had seen at Newport. He blew at his cigar until the end glowed bright red, then he held it very close to my eyes and when I attempted to turn my face away he held me steady with his hand in my hair.

"I can blind you," he said, "by pushing this cigar into your eyes."

"Believe me," I said. "I would tell you everything if I could."

Baeza blew smoke at me. "Or we could take you into the desert and watch you die of thirst . . . or we could simply take your balls off . . . make you into a nice little girl."

I sobbed again, much louder this time. "I would tell you if I could. Can't you see that?"

I felt a hand fondling my buttocks and my entrails dissolved. I fought against the table, trying to move my arms and legs but I was helpless.

"Do you know," said Baeza, "there are many in the streets here who would find your predicament most exciting, sexually I mean? We could sell tickets for you tonight, hundreds of them."

"The man you want was killed in London."

"Yes," said Baeza, "we know. But the Reverend needed a replacement and that replacement was you."

"I didn't even know Rapps," I said. "All I do know is he got killed and the cameraman hired me instead. Rapps might have sold the diamonds and banked the money. It could be anywhere."

"Yes, indeed," said Baeza, "but the Reverend is convinced that you have it . . . and that is good enough for me."

"The Reverend is wrong," I said. "I don't have the nerve."

Baeza raised a hand and a small cassette player appeared on the table close to my face. "Your wife thinks so too," he said; and the next moment I heard her voice, brisk and unreal.

"Oh you wouldn't get him to do that," she said, and I could see her with her back straight and her legs crossed. "He hasn't got the courage, moral or physical."

Another voice spoke but it was further away from the mike and I couldn't hear what it said.

My wife laughed. "Because he's been in the film business all his life and he's still an assistant . . . he hasn't got the guts to move on. Look at all these books, all about films. This collection of video tapes—films. Make-believe. He's always saying he'd like to be in features, make real stories, and what does he do? He makes crap. He only got this job in Los Angeles because someone was killed at the last minute. You should have heard him before he left . . . scared of flying, scared of meeting a big star like Deegan, scared of the crew. Don't bother offering him the job . . . he'll only turn it down . . . he's a guaranteed worm . . ."

Baeza switched off the machine and I twisted my head to look at him. "She's right," I said, "she's right."

Baeza nodded. "I am inclined to agree," he said, "but unfortunately there is so much money at stake that we cannot afford to take chances." He rose from his chair and someone else moved to my right-hand side. I twisted my head again and saw the glint of a hypodermic.

"No," I said, "please, no. I don't want to die . . . please. She told you the truth. I'm not worth the killing. I'm a nobody. I don't know . . ."

I felt the needle pierce my skin and what little self-control I had remaining broke down in despair. I screamed with all my might against death, my lungs bursting and my mouth stretched wide. Then my sobs became a moaning and my words incoherent.

But they weren't incoherent for me. I said all those things I had always hoped I'd never say, and they were the same things I'd always known I would say the first time I faced the threat of death: "Dear God, I'll do anything if you let me live just a little longer."

The last thing I saw was the big brass buckle on Baeza's wide belt. An embossed picture of a cowboy riding a bucking bronco. Slowly it went out of focus, then it shone brightly and became a beautiful golden sun, then it dulled and I fell into a big, deep sleep.

The Hollywood Takes 151

Coming back to consciousness was a long slow business. It started with a small, barely perceptible pin-point of light which gradually grew larger. I had no idea what the light was or who was watching it. It was just light. If I had a mind at all it was of a piece with the universe and there was no distinction between the two.

After what seemed an age the light spread and became stronger. My mind shrank and as it shrank a distant pain came nearer. A blinding headache made itself visible as jagged colours clashing inside my skull. Then my body defined itself, aching, the muscles tender. I groaned and was surprised at the loudness of the noise. I moved my tongue and it felt as rigid and as rough as a rasp.

I began to remember things next and for a while I held myself as still as I could. I had no wish to discover what they had done to me. Was I blind or not? How long had I been out—a day, a week, a month?

At last I found a smattering of courage and opened my eyes and a grey, early morning light filtered into them. I was lying on my back and shivering; every part of me was cold. I tried to sit up but could not move. I felt sick and the hot rush of vomit came, up from the deepest part of my stomach. I rolled onto my side but I was not quick enough and the stuff went all down me. I closed my eyes and pressed my face into the cold earth, breathing in short gasps to get as much oxygen into me as possible.

Earth? I opened my eyes once more and stared. An ant went by. There were one or two strands of grass, some pebbles and stones and shards of windscreen. I levered myself up from the floor as far as an elbow and looked about me.

I was in the burnt-out shell of a limousine which had

been dumped in the middle of an uneven square of terrain, rich in garbage—armchairs, stoves, tyres and beer cans. The square itself covered a large area and was bounded on all sides by unpaved roads. Along these roads stood the derelict shanties in which the poor of Los Angeles lived. When you hit the bottom of the pile this was where you came.

It was just after dawn and nothing stirred in the streets. I propped myself up against the back of the car, tore a strip of felt from the roof and tried to wipe the front of me clean. I wondered if I would be able to walk. What drug had they pumped into me? I might have been weeks in that house; perhaps I was already past help, with the seed of death growing within me. I had to make sure somehow. I had to get out of here and back to the hotel. For all I knew the others might have gone home in despair long since, leaving me alone and penniless. As the thought struck me I searched my pockets, but it was all there: the passport, money, hotel key, and credit card.

I came out of the carcass of the limousine on my hands and knees. I stayed that way for a while, shaking my head. Both halves of my jacket fell on either side of me, the trousers too. Four Mexican women went by on their way to work; they looked at me and looked away.

After a sustained effort I managed to get myself sitting on an old box and strung my jacket together with some bits of wire. For the trousers I ripped some of the sticky tape from my ankles and mended them that way. Then I swayed to my feet, fell once, got up again and began to shamble across the ground to the roadway.

I went into the street opposite me and a car went by, its springs screeching as it lurched over the rough surface of the ground. I followed in its direction, still stumbling and hoping I wouldn't be sick again. From time to time people came out of their houses, Mexicans. Some stared at me and shrugged their shoulders; others laughed.

The scenery didn't change as I went along. Board-built shacks everywhere, with patched roofs, and where there weren't patches there were just holes. The roadway was cracked and spilling over with dust and dirt, bricks and stones. Black car tyres lay here and there and slivers of glass shone between soft mounds of dog shit. Even in the early morning the stench shimmered all around me and above my head.

It was a long road and from time to time I had to stop and lean on a fence or a gate. At last I came to the end of it and found myself on some kind of boulevard or highway. There was a nameplate on the corner but it meant nothing to me. I waited. I hailed four or five cabs but they ignored me. I was just a bum with no money. That gave me the idea; I pulled a twenty-dollar bill from my pocket and held it in my hand and waved it. Soon a taxi pulled in but the driver didn't like the look of me. His nose wrinkled at the smell. I shoved the twenty into his hand and added another. "I was mugged," I said. "Please take me to the Treetops Hotel, it's up in North Hollywood."

After one more moment of reflection the driver nodded and I got into the cab. Here there was no partition and the back doors had handles. "You got today's paper," I asked.

"Sure," said the man, and threw it over. "I'm surprised you feel like reading."

I glanced at the dateline on the paper and my heart swelled with the joy of it. This early morning was the morning following the night of my attempted escape. I leant back in my seat and after all the fear, all the tension, I found myself alive again. Huge tears of relief tumbled down my cheeks and I could no longer control myself. I sobbed with happiness.

The taxi-driver looked into his mirror and I saw the concern on his face. "Boy," he said, "they sure must have worked you over. You see a doctor as soon as you get back . . . I'm counting on you, okay?"

Back at Treetops the cab took me past the reception area and I saw a police car still on duty there. We went on up to the little parking island outside pavilion seven and I tried to give my driver some more money but he refused.

"I'd like to ask you a question though," he said, his face creased in puzzlement. "How come them muggers left you all this money?"

"I had it in my sock," I said, giving the first answer that came to me.

The driver shook his head and then smiled. "Well, you sure was lucky. Them guys normally cut your feet off and keep the shoes and socks for later."

There was no policeman to be seen outside my door and I got into my room unnoticed. The tears of relief welled up again and I was none too successful at holding them back. I threw my clothes into a corner, ordered breakfast and ran a hot bath, tipping a half bottle of eau-de-cologne into it. I drank some mineral water from the fridge and when breakfast came I took the tray into the bathroom, got into the water and ate it there.

As the food and the hot water worked on me I began to feel better. In a funny way I felt that I'd achieved something; as if I'd been through fire and come out tempered, purged even. I was no braver than before, I would never be that, but I was no longer frightened either and I could see myself more clearly. The Mexicans had let me go, after one night. They must have decided that I had, after all, told the truth and that I was not worth the killing. At least I had that to be thankful for.

My wife had been quite correct in her description of me. Over the years what small ambitions I had attempted to nurture had always perished, dying from lack of daring and purpose. Now, at my age, I had no wish for anything other than the quiet life. I did not want to be noticed or threatened; I did not want to do great things, and those who did were not, in my experience, any better as human-beings than I was. Fate had made me a camera-assistant, not a diamond-smuggler or a private-eye. I did not want to walk down the mean streets of this or any other city. The heroes in the films of my youth had controlled their envi-ronment—I was controlled by mine. I was swept along by a powerful and dirty river, unable to swim against the current which was too strong for me. All I could do, all I wanted to do, was cling to the bit of timber that had been flung up against me and hang on for dear life, concerned only with keeping my head above water. That was enough effort for me.

The cow-bell in the phone jangled and I lifted my arm out of the water and reached for the receiver on the wall behind me.

"Hello," said Ernie, "sleep well?"

I hesitated for only a second before telling the lie, in-stinctively: "Yes, I did. Like a top."

"Good. I want to come round and get the gear. Nick and Ronnie and me are going to have a quick breakfast and then we're going to knock off these pick-ups and Gee-Vees."

"What about me?"

"Oh, we can manage," said Ernie. "A lot of it will be

from the car, and all the mags are loaded, aren't they? Anyway Tony wants you to go to the airport with him and Alex so that you can drop the limo at the car-hire place."

"Okay. What time?"

"I'll find out. Not before eleven I shouldn't think. I'll tell you when I come round for the gear."

I dropped the receiver back into its cradle and turned on the hot tap with my toes in order to relieve a slight chill in the bath-water. I had passed the Mexican test all on my own, but if I wanted to escape from Los Angeles, I would still have to meet the Reverend one more time. This was not a prospect I relished by any means but one I at last felt better able to face, and the sooner the better.

16

Sweet Smell of Success

At eleven o'clock I helped Tony and Alex load their bags into the limousine. There was so much luggage that the whole rear part of the car was full to the roof and the three of us had to sit together on the front seat.

"It's clothes mainly," said Tony, his greed appearing on his face as a grin, "and presents for the family."

I was still feeling pretty shaky from the night before so I was glad when Alex offered to drive. At the airport we left the limousine in the car park and a porter came with a trolley for the suitcases. Our goodbyes in the departure lounge were perfunctory; the director and the producer didn't like me very much and I couldn't stand either of them. I watched their heads in the crowd as they went through the gate to the "Passengers Only" area and I turned away with a sigh of relief.

I spent quite a while talking to the man in the car-hire office. I told him where the car was and gave him the keys. In return he told me where to pick up a cab for the journey back to Treetops. "It's a long ride," he said. "You'd better buy something to read."

I did not leave the airport concourse immediately. I bought myself a cup of coffee and then wandered and watched. I stood outside and looked at people arriving and departing—men with Stetsons and suntans and beautiful women. An announcement in English and Spanish, repeated every two minutes or so, told drivers they couldn't park in the white zone. The jets screamed and lowered themselves onto the runways. This was life in the fast lane, the car-stickers said. I didn't know which lane I'd been travelling in but it had certainly been a bumpy ride.

I walked around for a little longer and bought a copy of the Los Angeles *Times*—then I could put it off no longer. I was remembering the advice of the girl who'd taken me to the Church of God's Will that first time. I knew the Reverend would not allow me to leave Los Angeles without talking to me at least once more. It would be better, I thought, if I went looking for him instead of hoping that he would forget all about me.

Right at the end of the concourse was a large stand with a white-and-blue banner above it which said, "Welcome to Los Angeles and the Church of God's Will. The Reverend J. Turrill." It was here that those arriving in Los Angeles for the first time, especially if they had nowhere to go, could seek advice and practical help. The Church of God's Will would take them in, comfort them, provide them with a ready-made social circle and give them somewhere to sleep. It was a good idea and it worked. Hundreds of the Reverend's followers were fished in this way.

Behind the stand were a young man and a young woman. They were dressed in clean, crisp clothes and their faces were bright and shiny with love and confidence. I approached them and leant against the counter. They both smiled warmly.

"Yes," said the young man.

"I need to speak to the Reverend."

A look of concern came over their faces. "The Reverend

doesn't often have time to answer individual queries," said the young man. "That's what we do."

"Yes, I know," I answered, "but I have met him twice already and I think that today he will want to talk to me."

"I'll phone him at the village," said the girl. She picked up a white phone and began making a number. "Your name?"

I gave her my name and while we waited I took up a brochure, read it and put it in my pocket. After a while the girl spoke, waited again and then spoke to someone else. Eventually she blushed deeply and handed me the receiver.

"It's the Reverend himself," she said, as if announcing God.

"Hello," I said. The young man and the girl moved away respectfully.

The Reverend answered and asked me how I was.

"Better than I expected to be this morning," I said, and drew a breath. "Reverend, I am supposed to be leaving for England tomorrow and I thought you would want to see me before I go. I mean I don't know anymore than I did . . . but I just wondered . . . you know?"

"It's perfectly all right now," said the Reverend. "Certain matters have been resolved and it won't be necessary for us to meet again. But I must admit you have surprised me. I am rarely mistaken in my judgement of men but I seem to have been wrong about you. There is nothing more to say except may God be with you . . . enjoy your trip home."

At this the line went dead, not that I would have been able to say anything anyway; I was overcome with relief. With those few words the Reverend had restored me to myself; my life was my own again.

I must have been smiling seraphically for the young cou-

ple behind the counter came close and smiled seraphically
too, shaking their heads slowly in astonishment at my having spoken to the prophet himself.

"Isn't it wonderful," said the girl, "talking to him . . .
the effect he has, even on the telephone—the holiness that
comes from him."

I blinked my eyes like someone coming round from a
knock-out blow. "Yes," I said. "The holiness."

Still dazed I walked away from them, retracing my steps
along the concourse and heading towards the exit doors,
passing the airline desks on my way. A ground hostess in
the red livery of Atlantic-Pacific-Airways came into view
and fell into step beside me.

"Aren't you one of the guys staying at Treetops and
shooting a film out here?"

I was still so high from the brief conversation I'd had
with the Reverend that I did not answer the question. I did
not even realize that anyone was talking to me until the
words were repeated.

I turned to face her. "I'm sorry. Yes I am."

She tightened her lips and moved her head from side to
side. "I thought you were when those two checked in just
now. Wouldn't you believe it? Here's that unit manager of
yours making a production about some bag that was mis-
routed when you arrived and here's me making calls all
over, from Heathrow to Tokyo, so when it comes in from
Auckland I can't raise any of you at the hotel. They said
you were at the airport."

"Bag," I said, still numb.

"If you come with me and sign for it, you can take it
away."

I followed the girl to the desk and signed a receipt. She
watched me closely as I wrote, as if overjoyed to see the

completion of a particularly onerous task. Then she took
the piece of paper and went to a cupboard and brought
from it Rapps's green canvas ditty-bag, the one I had not
seen since the baggage men had loaded it into the plane at
Heathrow.

"Here," she said, giving it to me, "take it away and
make sure you tell Ronnie. I don't want him calling me
again."

I thanked the girl and went through the nearest exit
doors. I had taken two hits in the space of five minutes and
my mind was reeling. People knocked me out of their way
as they rushed to their planes, but unaware of my surroundings, I did not notice their rudeness. I hugged the
bag to my chest and shuffled forward, crossing the access
road blindly and making several cars blast their horns.
Safely over I went into the parking lot, walking until I
found a quiet bench to sit on. I needed time to think.

After a few minutes I came out of my trance and peered
into the bag. It was all there: camera tape, screwdrivers,
torches, felt tips, even the small clapper-board and the golf
balls that Rapps had bought for Ernie—a dozen of them
still neatly packed in their box.

I took the box of golf balls in my hand and stood to look
around. I turned slowly in a full circle and gazed across
the rows of car roofs. A jet throttled back above my head.
I saw no one; no one at any rate who was showing the least
interest in me.

I sat once more on the bench and took from the ditty-
bag the largest screwdriver and a sharp knife. I chose a
golf ball at random and cut a slot into it. Then I placed it
on the ground between my feet, inserted the end of the
screwdriver into the slot and, using all my strength and
weight, began to bore a way through.

It was slow, hard work and the golf ball did not drop open as I had half-imagined it would. Eventually the screwdriver bit on the ground beneath and I held up the ball and looked into it. I blew the dust away and looked again. Nothing. I raked inside it with a smaller screwdriver and banged the ball against the arm of the bench. Again nothing.

I tried six more of the golf balls in this way and by the time I gave up I had a sore spot in my right palm that would soon be a blister—but I had no diamonds, not a single one. I swore; as if finding ten million dollars would be that easy. I threw my tools back into the bag.

The bag! Even in diamonds ten million dollars would take up quite a lot of space. Rapps had been straight about the golf balls—they had been for Ernie, but everything else in the bag, and the bag itself, was suspect. The long, thick shoulder strap, the circular wooden bottom, the double seams, the cans of anti-flare, the felt-tips and especially the clapper-board—they could all be carrying contraband.

I reached into the bag again, took out the clapper-board and held it in front of me. It was approximately twelve inches by nine, which was normal, but it was also about three inches thick, which wasn't.

I turned it over but saw nothing suspicious. I shook it close to my ear but heard no noise. I tapped it with my knuckle and it sounded solid. I turned it over again, looking at the bottom, and at last began to think I might be right this time, for although the board had been heavily painted in black, at each end of this bottom side I could see a small circle showing through the surface of the paint.

I took out my knife again and with the point of it I scraped until I had removed a plug of plastic wood and revealed the head of a counter-sunk brass screw. I did the same at the other end with the same result. Trembling with excitement I undid the screws, and with the help of a little leverage, the length of wood which formed the lower side of the clapper-board came away.

My excitement had been premature. All I could see now was an uneven strip made from a quantity of hardened putty. It had been used to fill the long gap between the two sides and also painted black. I cut at it with the knife and it began to flake away. Soon I had uncovered a wire mesh that must have been tacked into position to receive the putty when still soft. Once I had disposed of that I saw that the clapper-board was indeed hollow, and appeared to be tightly stuffed with cotton wool.

It wasn't. I pulled at the first layer and it proved to be the only one. Underneath it were scores of diamonds, hundreds of them for all I knew, packed so closely together they couldn't move. So Rapps had not done the dirty. He had probably loaded the whole bag, and perhaps its contents also, in the same way. And it was more than likely that he had not set out to deceive the Reverend but had died because he had crossed the road carelessly—and I had suffered what I had suffered as a result of the same accident.

Gingerly, for diamonds are sacred, I took one of the largest between thumb and forefinger and held it up against the sun. Even I could see that it had been beautifully cut and the deep, cold fire of it burnt into my retina. I squinted, blind with greed and my joy grew until I thought my body would not retain it. If all that the Reverend had said was true, then I had ten million dollars' worth of diamonds in my hands. If I wished I could be a Deegan or a Tony Maretta ten times over. The money that made all things possible was mine—and nobody knew I had it.

17

Wonder Man

The idea of being a multi-millionaire was a seductive one and for a little while it warmed me and made me happy. But such an idea could not survive long in my mind and what was more I knew it all the time. A lack of daring was not something that came and went in my psyche—it was part of my flesh and blood, it made me tick.

I held the diamond against the sky once again and observed how the light within it was cold and implacable. Five men had already died for this wealth and I had no wish to be the sixth. Even if I summoned up my courage and kept the diamonds, I knew I would not be allowed to enjoy them. The Reverend had men in London already. The slightest change in my life-style would be noted and one night someone would come to see me and I would have a lot of talking to do.

I could run for it, of course. Change my name and move to Venezuela. I laughed. I couldn't do that either. I'd rather live poor than be chased around the world for years, only to be caught in the end.

I sighed and looked out over the car park. I was still alone. The planes came and went above me and the announcement about not parking in the white zone went on and on. Perhaps I should have taken the ditty-bag to the police and told them the whole story. The money had obviously been come by illegally, untaxed, taken from some account in Switzerland, then transferred to Amsterdam and laundered into diamonds for easy transportation. After all, they took up no space and were negotiable anywhere.

And what would the cops do if I arrived on their doorstep with ten million dollars' worth of somebody else's loot? Even if they prosecuted the Reverend, there was little doubt that his lawyers would protect him. I had no proof of a connection between him and the diamonds, and the only man who once had, Rapps, was dead.

The luxury of upright behaviour was not for me. Informing the police would make the Reverend very angry, and as he'd said, angry people do violent things. And the Mexicans might also come after me, and not just to slap me on the back by way of congratulation.

There was only one thing I could do if I wanted to return to the quiet life I prized so much. I had better visit the Reverend immediately, tell him what had happened and hand over the diamonds. He might use the money for good, he might use it for evil—that didn't matter, not to me it didn't. Only one thing was my concern—survival.

I looked at the diamond I held for one last time and decided against slipping it into my pocket. I put it away with the others and stuffed in the cotton wool, which I then stuck into place with a strip of camera tape. Last of all I screwed the length of wood back into position. When I'd finished I shouldered the ditty-bag, walked towards the taxi-rank and gave the brochure I'd picked up earlier to a cab-driver, pointing to a picture of the Reverend's village.

"I want to go there," I said.

The cabbie looked. "Okay," he answered, "but it's a long way."

I got into the back of the car. "I don't give a damn," I said. "I can afford it."

The cabbie was right and we drove for many miles. I paid no attention to the route we took—all I remember is that we headed west, into the hills, not stopping until we came to a security gate set in a fence where four armed men kept watch. I wound down my window and told them that I wanted to see the Reverend, and no one else. I waited while one of the men made a phone call but as soon as he put down the receiver he smiled, the gate was opened and I was driven forward.

The road inside the fence was metalled but narrow. The grass on either side was burnt dry and short by the summer sun and there were no trees. Then we crossed a low ridge, came down into a shallow valley and everything changed.

The valley must have been nine or ten miles long and about five wide. It had been regularly watered and as the cab advanced I could see high garden jets everywhere, whipping round in vast circles, making instant rainbows that appeared for a split second only and then folded into the ground. Scores of sycamores and firs had been planted at proper intervals and underneath and between them spread a rich carpet of grass sown with bright flowers.

It was a tidy landscape, surprising out here in surroundings of barrenness, but what was even more surprising was that all along the road, and down the side roads also, small houses had been built, hundreds of them. And they had been built with great care, so as to blend with the scenery —wooden frames with wide porches, thatched roofs and clusters of trees nearby, leaning over to shade tables and chairs.

Some of the houses had cars outside, and all had bicycles and electric buggies like the ones at the golf club. As my cab went by, people came to their windows and porches to wave and many of them were clad in loose-fitting caftans of different colours, robes that dropped from the shoulder to the ankle, leaving the body cool and free. Those not dressed in this way were simply wearing shorts and sweat-shirts, just like anyone else in California.

"Well, hell," said the cabbie. "I heard about it a lot but it sure is bigger than I thought."

The road brought us at length to an administration building constructed from the same materials as the houses we had passed, although it was several times larger. It had been designed on a different plan too, being hexagonal in shape and rising to three storeys.

The cab halted and I got out into the sun, taking my bag with me. The cabbie poked his head from the car and whistled and I could understand why. As far as the eye could see the neat roads radiated away from this central position and the grass and the trees and the houses covered the whole valley. This was the Reverend's village—a dream coming true.

The ground floor of the building in front of me was open on all sides and was used as a garage for the twenty or so cars that stood there, sheltered in the shade. An open staircase rose to the first floor, and after asking the driver to wait for me, I went towards it and began to climb.

I arrived on a wide landing and stepped down into an airy room which occupied all the space available on this floor. It was laid out in the same manner as the large office at the Church of God's Will back in Los Angeles. There were desks here and there and at each one a group of people worked together at computer terminals and telephones. The windows were all open and beyond them was a spacious balcony and I could see splendid views in every direction. To one side of the room was a desk larger than the others and behind it sat the Reverend himself, dressed in a splendid caftan of his own.

As I entered the Hexagon, two men stepped from each side of the entrance, smiled pleasantly and asked me to sit down. One of them took my bag, looked inside, then gave it back to me. A young girl brought me a drink of iced lemonade, made from real lemons, and I noticed that a glass was taken down to the taxi-driver also.

I waited for about half an hour until I was conducted, with more smiles, to the Reverend's desk, where a comfortable armchair had been placed for me. As I sat, the Reverend's assistants withdrew to a respectful distance and I placed my ditty-bag on the floor. The Reverend joined his hands together and spoke in that deep rich voice of his. Once again I could understand why they followed him and why they lived his way. Even I felt proud to be alone with him.

"I didn't expect to see you," he said, as if the privilege were his, "but I am pleased you took the trouble to visit us. Now you can see how we do things."

I took a sip from my lemonade and placed the glass on the desk. The Mexicans had finished with me and the Reverend himself had said I could go home. I felt free to say things.

"I came to wish you goodbye," I began, "but I also wanted to ask a couple of questions before I left."

The Reverend raised his hands in a gesture of permission.

"How is it that you don't care if I leave town any more. I have consistently told you the truth. Why is it you suddenly believe me?"

The Reverend rose and stood to his full height, his great bulk disguised by the loose robe. Effortlessly he moved round the desk and someone brought him a chair. He lowered his body into it easily and the desk was no longer between us—an exercise in charm.

"I owe you a confession and an apology," he said, "and I hope, when I have explained, you will forgive and understand. The business of our church is of prime importance to us, that is our excuse and it is the only one I offer . . . you see I knew the Mexicans had taken you . . . I arranged it. I also know what happened and what was said."

I went to ask a question but the Reverend raised a clean pink hand and I fell silent.

"Now you have seen the village you will realize why the diamonds are so important to me and, at the same time, to my enemies. They want this place destroyed and to starve me of capital is the best way to do it. Life is a war between good and evil and I have to use all the weapons available to me. I have a man placed amongst the Mexicans, a faithful member of my Church. I knew of my enemy's intentions the very moment their decisions were made. Once they had learnt of my interest in you they decided to interrogate you, so I decided to allow them to perform a disagreeable task that I had no wish to perform myself. On the night of your interrogation the room was bugged and my men were not far away, listening to every word that was said."

"I might have been killed."

The Reverend smiled. "Yes. But then for all I knew you were a man attempting to steal ten million dollars from me and such a man could be no ordinary person. I needed to find out what you were made of, so did they. I needed you isolated, broken, as near death as made no difference. I wanted the truth to come pouring out. Only a professional could have withstood what you were put through. Your very ordinariness saved your life and there is no reason for you to feel ashamed."

"And that recording of my wife's voice?"

The Reverend shook his head by way of regret. "It must have been very disagreeable for you. They have men over there, they wanted to be sure about you."

"If I'd had the diamonds," I said, rushing the words out, "I would have told them. Wasn't that a risk for you?"

"I was prepared," said the Reverend. "They would not have made it as far as their cars."

"You still haven't got the diamonds. One of the others on the crew might have flown out with them."

The Reverend raised his hands again, admitting the possibility. "Perhaps. In any event, they will be watched for a long while and if their habits change . . ."

I swallowed a lump in my throat. "I thought so," I said.

The Reverend went on with his explanation. "The man, Rapps, had done a lot of work for me, and there was always a fail-safe plan. If for any reason he could not come on a trip himself he had a replacement ready. I thought it was you—we had to make sure it wasn't. It was conceivable that you had been tempted by the amount of money involved as Rapps obviously was. The loss of the diamonds is a disaster for our Church but we will survive it. Knowing that we are on the side of good is a more powerful weapon than money even." The Reverend permitted himself a weak smile. "I am, however, still annoyed at being mistaken about you. I was convinced you were the man. It is a feeling I have about people and up until now it has never been wrong."

I blushed but kept going. "One last thing. I was injected with something last night. Can your Mexican friend find out what it was? I could have something very nasty running round my veins."

"Please calm your mind," said the Reverend. "It was a truth drug with only minor side-effects . . . and the needle was clean. It was my man that administered it."

"Only a truth drug," I said, and I smiled broadly and the Reverend joined his smile to mine—two felonious and successful companions. Such a man! Using his enemies to find out the facts and listening to the results at his leisure.

I finished my lemonade and took the clapper-board and a screwdriver from my ditty-bag. I looked at the Reverend as I undid the two screws and he looked straight back at me. He knew what was coming. When the strip of wood came away I threw it onto the desk, ripped out the camera tape and cotton wool and, very gently, poured the diamonds onto the desk top. Slowly the Reverend rose to his feet and slowly the noise of work around us ceased. The whole Hexagon became silent. A solitary phone rang then stopped as someone lifted the receiver and laid it down.

The Reverend looked at the diamonds but did not touch them. Greed was not one of his failings. He looked at me in wonderment and now that I had played my little scene I felt shy, embarrassed. I blushed again. He raised a hand to summon someone from behind him. "You are no ordinary man," he said.

"But I am," I replied. "It's just the way things turned out." I wanted to explain more but at that moment one of the Reverend's acolytes came forward, bidden by the raised hand, scooped up the diamonds and replaced them inside the clapper-board.

"Take the bag upstairs," said the Reverend, then he faced the people in the room, put his arm around my shoulders and shook me softly, in a loving way, and everyone in that room smiled at me and loved me too.

"This man," and the Reverend's voice was no longer caressing but hard and strong, "this man has performed a service for this Church unequalled by any of us. He has been brave, he has been steadfast and he deserves the love and admiration of you all. I shall ask him to join us."

With these words the Reverend removed his arm from me and, quietly, began to clap his hands. The tension in the room broke and all those present smiled at me again and clapped their hands also. I stared at my feet and tears rose to my eyes. To be admired by so many people! Nothing like this had ever happened to me before.

18

Sentimental Journey

When the applause had died away, the Reverend steered me up another flight of stairs and into his private apartments. Again, as at the Church, the available space was equally divided between one large area and several small rooms, though here the furnishings suggested relaxation rather than work, for there were couches and armchairs dotted all over a floor that was covered in fine Persian rugs.

I followed the Reverend onto the balcony and we sat together at a big wooden table where two places were already laid. Far below I could see an enormous swimming-pool filled with bright blue water. There were people in the pool and parasols all around it. Occasionally a shout or the splash of a body diving rose to us and I thought I saw my taxi driver watching things with his hands dug deep into his pockets. No sooner had we sat than food was brought to us by two or three young people, who said nothing but placed the dishes on the table and retired out of earshot.

The Reverend offered me some bread. There was, I noticed, no meat on the table. Only vegetables, fruit, various cheeses and a variety of salads.

"What delights me most," said the Reverend, "is that my flair has been proved correct. I knew I was right about you all along, and now events have proved it. It makes me very content."

I tried to explain. "It just turned up at the airport," I said. "I didn't even know where the bag was."

The Reverend would have none of this and waved my words away. He wanted his original feeling about me to be the true one and he would allow nothing to alter that state of affairs. "No more of that," he said, giving a strangely infectious laugh. "There are more serious things to be talked of. What are your plans?"

"I have none. I want to go home, that's all. Lead the life I led before."

The Reverend pointed a finger at me. "Life will never be the same for you, not now that you have been here and done what you have done. Did you have some coded message sent back to England so that the bag was freighted out to you at the right time?"

"Nothing like that."

The Reverend passed me a bowl of salad. "Let it be your secret, but at least allow me to admire your bravery and your timing . . . and your acting ability. Those who employ the Mexicans to work against me will have been convinced, as I was, that the diamonds are still in Europe. They think me without funds, unable to act. Now I shall surprise them . . . soon they will be running for their lives. You have put me in a very strong position."

I made one more attempt, albeit a very weak one, to convince the Reverend that I was not responsible for what had happened but he would not listen and so I abandoned the idea for ever and ate my lunch. As I ate, my companion talked.

"I have asked you to eat with me today," he began, "because I want you to listen to me, very seriously. I would like you to join me. I want you to come here to live, with your wife and children if you wish, without them if you prefer . . ." He held up his hand as I went to answer.

"Do not answer yet. A man like you could be very happy here, and there would be much for you to do. These people, these members of my Church, they are not bound here, they come and go as they please, many work in Los Angeles and in other places. What they earn and what they learn out in the world is of great value to our campaign. But they return here to find the peace of mind that we all need."

I nodded and helped myself to a slice of melon.

"There is another thing," continued the Reverend. "The man Rapps was to have been well paid for bringing the diamonds to me. He would have received enough to make him independent for the rest of his life. That money is of course now yours, if you want it. There will be no more need for you to work at anything that does not please you. Here, in Los Angeles, you could help me. Courage and cunning like yours are qualities I need."

I picked at some salad with my fork. "Moving to California," I said, "is something that I would have to think about."

The Reverend smiled his understanding and I hesitated for a moment before going on. Being taken for a person with courage was making me bold and in this new character I felt I could say anything, and so I affected a high moral tone, though I knew that it was not virtue that spurred me forward but common or garden curiosity.

"This money," I said, "diamonds, it's not just tax evasion, is it? It's importing drugs, and selling them."

The Reverend's eyes hardened for a second, then he relaxed as he came to his decision. "If you join my Church,"

he said, "as I hope you will, you will have to understand
the philosophy that inspires us . . . so there is no reason
why you should not hear some of it now, and as far as I am
concerned you have earned the right." He stretched forward and poured me a tall glass of orange juice and made
himself comfortable as if for a long speech.

"I started with encounter groups, in a very small way. I
had found my road and I wanted to show others how to
find God. I gave courses and took nothing more than a
reasonable donation. I helped people find their true selves
and slowly I built my Church. But we were small and
powerless and I knew it wasn't enough. We were kind,
genteel—and weak. My Church was a tiny yellow flame on
the edge of an endless black night. In my heart I knew it
was not meant to be like that. The world had not been
created for the benefit of the powers of evil.

"After many days and nights of thinking, the answer,
when it came, was simple. We did not fight hard enough.
We were too easy-going, more concerned with manners
than results, more worried about our image than the de-
fence of our ideals. Suddenly I became tired of being for
ever on the losing side. I decided to change things. I decided to win."

I picked up an apple and began to peel it. The Reverend
went on, his eyes of stone beginning to shine.

"I studied the powers of evil. I learnt how they work.
That, too, was simple. Evil uses every weapon it can, it
destroys without remorse, then it consolidates and
camouflages itself in respectability. All I did was to adopt
these tactics and employ them in the service of good. To
do so I needed power and power is merely money. It didn't
matter how this money was obtained, you understand, as
long as the result of using it was good."

"But how do you know you're right?"

"How do I know? Because man is predestined to die, predestined for hell or heaven. He will follow the road that has been marked for him. Only the elect are free. They understand that the God who governs the universe is not blind, nor is he helpless. They understand his will and they work with it; that is why they are permitted to fight hard in the way of this world and yet still inherit the next. We have the best, the only, reason for making money—we use it to fight evil."

"And the three union men, the Mexican hanging from the Hollywood sign, the people who die along the way. What about them?"

The Reverend raised a finger as if explaining to a child. "You have obviously never heard of the concept of the 'just war.' Didn't the ancient archbishops ride out to battle wielding two-handed swords to slay the infidel?"

"I don't know a lot about religion," I said, "but dealing in drugs, that must be wrong."

The Reverend rested his hands on the table top, and I stopped eating to listen to him. The two or three people who had served the meal came nearer, soundlessly, their faces radiant, approaching the well of truth. I sipped at my orange juice and the Reverend went on.

"The problem of evil has always plagued the theologian," he said, "until now, but there is no real problem once we understand God's purpose. If evil is to be eradicated then the men of good will, the elect, must turn the power of evil against itself. All the world's pain and distress comes from the fact that we temporize, we pretend that we can change evil into good. We cannot, but we can eradicate it wherever we see it. There have always been religious wars and millions have died in them, innocent and guilty. At this time we are fighting in the greatest war of all, and in this war it doesn't matter a bit how many addicts or tramps or free-loaders die, especially when they are damned already. Their going cleanses the earth and they die for the ultimate good."

I composed my face into an expression of wisdom. "And this ultimate good, will we ever see it?"

The Reverend waved an arm towards the valley. "We are seeing it now, and that is because we are at last fighting the war we should have been fighting all these years. Believe me, there are people within, and beyond, the borders of this country who want to destroy our way of life entirely, but God would not have gone to the trouble of creating the universe just to see it conquered by his enemies. This is a great country, the greatest, but it has lost its way. It needs to be shown a new frontier, a frontier that is spiritual. Like in the old days we will have to fight violence with violence for a while but then we need to cut away the dead wood and burn it. We must make room for a new forest to grow. A new country, fine and brave, will leap out of the earth and there will be villages like this one all over the world."

I looked out from the balcony where I sat, and I gazed down the valley. My brain could take no more. "I don't know," I said. "You make it sound so simple."

The Reverend laid his hand on my bare forearm and I could feel his strength as it burned into my body, filling me with new blood.

"There is so much for us to do," he said, "and I search for men and women who possess the qualities needed in war. That is why there is a place for you here, and there always will be. I want you to know that."

I thanked the Reverend for his confidence in me and as I

did two of his acolytes came forward from where they'd been listening and began to clear away the remains of the meal.

"If things had turned out differently," I asked, "would you have locked me up in that hospital of yours after all?"

The Reverend's face became sombre. "If it furthered the cause of the Church," he said, "I would do anything. If you had indeed stolen the money and your death would have brought it back, then you would have died."

I swallowed at the old familiar lump in my throat, but I went on. "Is it really a hospital?"

"Oh yes, we manage to save some. For others it is simply a quiet place to die."

With this the Reverend stood and that was the end of it. He had given me enough of his time and the gaze of the acolytes told me that I had been more than usually honoured.

"Before I go," I said, "I have been thinking about the money you were going to give Rapps, and I'm grateful, really, but you see although I like the idea of a lot of money I don't like the idea of money that comes from drugs . . . it may be the only scruple I have but there it is, so perhaps you could use it for some good thing. I don't know, something in the hospital, say."

It took me a great deal of effort to make this little speech and I did not feel brave or particularly saintly while it was going on. It sprang from no moral conviction; it was nothing more than a reflex—what the Reverend might have called a romantic lack of realism.

Whatever his opinion the Reverend kept it to himself. "We are shortly to extend our hospital here," he said. "I shall see that a ward is named after you. Now you must excuse me. With the arrival of the diamonds I have much

to do. One of my limousines will take you back to Los
Angeles. I don't expect any more trouble but I shall ask
some of my people to stay with you until you leave. One
last thing. I would like you to visit someone before you go.
It may help you to make up your mind about joining us.
Please remember the gates here are always open for you.
For my part I feel sure that I shall see you again, and as
you know, I am rarely mistaken."

This remark made both of us smile. We shook hands and
I felt his power again. Then two young men, whose duty it
was, led me across the room, out onto the staircase and
down to ground level. There I saw that my taxi had gone
and in its place one of the Reverend's stretches was waiting for me. A door was opened, I got into the car and
without a word of command it swung round in a huge arc
and took me away from the Hexagon, heading along one
of the many radial roads at a sedate speed, and as I
watched, the trees went slowly by.

We drove for ten minutes or so and then the stretch
stopped.

"You want this one," said the driver through the intercom. "Twenny-twenny-nine."

I opened my door and got out of the air-conditioning. In
front of me was a narrow path rising gently across the
grass and leading towards one of the village houses. A mail
box on my left said two thousand and twenty-nine. I
walked up the path and a woman in one of the cotton
caftans appeared on the porch and raised an arm to greet
me. I should have known. It was Angela.

I mounted the steps and we sat on canvas chairs. On the
table between us were drinks and Angela poured me a
glass of something. I don't know what.

"Angela," I said, making no attempt to be original, "so you didn't go to Waterlooville?"

Angela shook her head and her hair swayed across her face. She looked content and sure of herself. Her eyes were frank and she gazed at me in open admiration, something I noticed immediately because no woman, or man for that matter, had ever looked at me in that way, before today.

"No," she answered, "I never intended to."

I nodded. I understood it all now. The old Del would have felt betrayed, frightened in retrospect. The new one didn't care. Angela tried a smile on me, saw that it worked and took my hand in hers.

"You set me up," I said. "The taxi was the Reverend's idea."

"Yes," said Angela, "it was. We had to know the truth and we thought we did . . . but in the end you fooled us all . . . you were brilliant."

"Yes, it wasn't easy. So you've been in the Church all along? Never left it?"

"All along, ever since I came from Iowa and hit rock bottom."

I looked at the bruises, still pale yellow on her face. "And those?"

"Oh, the Mexicans beat me up all right. They knew I was in the Church. I talked and told them what I believed . . . that you were the man they wanted."

"How can you be so certain . . . about the Reverend?"

Angela squeezed my hand. "Just by looking at the work he has done. He has saved so many people."

"What about those who don't make it, the ones that die, like Ermal and the others, and those that die of drugs?"

"God decides, Del. They are with him now or they are not. We have no option but to fight and soldiers get killed.

But look at the goodness that has come out of the Reverend's work. I know, Del. I was at the bottom of the pile. I would have killed my mother for a shot of heroin. It was the Reverend who saved me."

"Is there anything to stop you leaving here?"

Angela laughed. "I don't want to leave. Leave for what? I've never been happier. Sure I thought I was going to be a star when I got here. So do they all, and most of them end up as garbage—their lives wasted, their hopes gone in drink if they're lucky, in drugs if they're not. This work is real, Del. It means something. We do good here. Join with us, Del. Join with us and see."

"I'm going home tomorrow," I said. "Though the Reverend said I could come back any time . . . thinks I will too."

"He called me just now, said you were coming. He is so impressed, Del, with what you did. That money means a new village and he wants you with him. Oh, Del, come back soon. I know he would like it . . . and so would I."

Here Angela stood and grasping both my hands in hers she pulled me to my feet. The wide sleeves of her gown fell back and the coolness of her revealed arms encircled my neck. "I want you," she said, and kissed me on the mouth like I'd never been kissed before. Then she smiled at me with a smile so fresh that it might have been the first one she'd ever used.

"You've got to come back," she said, and taking my hand she pulled me into the house and we crossed the sitting-room and, still hand in hand, we went into the bedroom.

I left the house two hours later. I was dazed and found it difficult to put two thoughts together. It was as if I'd been suddenly thrust from dusk to daylight. I was still blinking and I couldn't even remember which way was up.

Angela came to the porch with me and kissed me one last goodbye.

"I'll be here," she whispered, just as they should in the last reel, and I went down the path.

My driver came out of the stretch and when I saw the book in his hand I apologised for keeping him waiting.

"It's an honour, sir," he said. "Besides, I've been catching up on my studies," and with that I got into the car and he closed the door behind me.

I waved once at Angela as we pulled away and then reclined on the wide seat. I looked out of the window. The roads and the houses stretched away on either side and there were more people to be seen than previously, standing in front of their houses. Suddenly I realized. It was me they were waiting for.

As the car passed they waved and clapped their hands and their children jumped up and down. In the next moment we had turned into a broader avenue, lined with tall sycamores. Here there were yet more people, long ranks of them by the edge of the road. The window in front of my face sunk noiselessly into the body of the car and I heard the wind going by and the sound of voices, and there were hands clapping.

"What's going on?" I asked.

"They want to thank you for what you've done, sir," answered the driver. "The Reverend has no secrets from us and so the word has gotten round."

For the second time that day tears pricked at my eyes. This—for my benefit—was the Reverend's last great scene. I could almost see THE END in letters a hundred feet high on the nearest hillside. I could almost hear the music as

the studio orchestra played its heart out on the sound
stage. The last ounce of sentiment was being wrung from
the movie with that merciless strength possessed only by
Hollywood. There wouldn't be a dry eye in the house—dry
eyes were not allowed.

I am quite sure that had I been a native-born American,
as distinct from one who had only been adopted by its
cinema, I would have ordered the car to turn around then
and there. As it was, I did nothing. Although I felt that
my character had changed to a certain degree, I was still
not ready for positive thought followed immediately by
definite action.

Something else stopped me too. I could not forget that
behind every great "weepie," grossing millions at the box-
office, sat a hard-nosed producer counting the money. So I
let the car go on, on through the applauding crowds that
were there only for me, out of the grass-covered valley,
through the gates and back towards Los Angeles. And the
events of those last few days got to me and all I could do
was sit and let the tears pour unhindered down my cheeks.
I was just another sucker, in an audience of suckers, who'd
paid good money for his seat just so that he could have a
good cry, all alone in the dark.

19

A Streetcar Named Desire

Going back to Treetops was like entering a foreign country, and eating that last dinner with Nick and Ernie was like eating with strangers.

Not that it was their fault. They were in high spirits, cheered by the thought of leaving Los Angeles, and my moody silences did not effect them. They had done their pick-up shots, put Ronnie on a plane and had spent a hilarious afternoon shopping for souvenirs.

"You asked me to get some stuff for your kids," said Nick. "I got stacks."

The rest of the evening went by slowly. We had a few drinks in the bar and then went to our rooms in order to pack.

At breakfast I told them about the stretch and the escort that would take us to the airport, in case the Mexicans planned a different sort of farewell. We could see the men and the cars through the big window, waiting for us just where the union men had waited.

"I'm impressed," said Ernie. "What did you have to do —write them a new hymn?"

When it was time for us to go the porters brought our luggage to the front of reception and the Reverend's men stowed it all into the three cars. Then we waved goodbye to the receptionists and the waiters and left Treetops for ever, a little cortege of three large limousines, the stretch in the middle.

"This is great," said Nick. "It's like being a mega-star." I noticed how tired he looked. "I was up all night," he explained, touching his face. "Waterbed. When I get to New Orleans I'm going to have a holiday."

At the airport the men saw to our tickets and all the luggage. Everyone smiled when they saw who was looking after us. Nick came to the gate to say goodbye; his flight was an hour later than ours.

"See you in London," he said, and we walked away from him and that was it. I was out of Los Angeles.

As soon as the sign came up, Ernie undid his seat-belt. "Am I glad to be up here," he said. "How about two large gin and tonics?"

"I went out to see that religious guy yesterday," I said. "He's got this village out in the hills, a big place. He offered me a job. Said I could live out there, money no object."

Ernie drew his breath in over his teeth and made a noise of disapproval. "What kind of a job?"

"Administration, I suppose."

Ernie looked out of his window and took in Arizona with a sweep of his eye. "It's up to you. It's a hard country to live in, America."

"We're all American now, Ernie."

Ernie grunted. "I'm not," he said, and closed his eyes.

I fell silent. Maybe I wasn't cut out for Los Angeles. But then I wasn't sure I wanted what I was going back to either: making training videos for insurance companies, trying to survive a dead marriage in a terraced house in

Mortlake. Compared to that, the world of sunny beaches, stretch automobiles and Angela stepping out of her loose robe seemed pretty good.

I let Ernie go to sleep and ordered myself another gin. I didn't really want to think any more but I couldn't stop it coming. I swore. Why had I refused the money that had been due to Rapps? Enough to make me independent for life, the Reverend had said. The only moral stand I had ever taken and I had taken it when there'd been a fortune at stake.

And I was more than sure that it was a decision I'd made for the wrong reasons. It had been the old cowardice again. I'd been scared of what so much money might do to me, scared that if I suddenly possessed money like that I would have no excuse for not doing those things I'd always said I would do as soon as I had the money. Money would batter down the walls of the rut I lived in and let in the light and the fresh air—two things I wasn't used to.

I got out of the taxi in my cul-de-sac, paid the man and watched him reverse his car back to the main road. Everything looked so small, the houses, everything. A train went by and the ground trembled a little. It was cold for July and the sunlight was pale, disappearing all the time as the clouds went by.

The place was empty when I got into it. There was bread and butter on the kitchen table and toys on the stairs. I went into the bedroom and put the suitcase onto the unmade bed and took out the things I'd got for the kids.

I began to unpack slowly, putting the dirty washing into the raffia bin in the corner. The clean stuff I put into the wardrobe.

I heard the key in the front door so I called out and the kids came running up the stairs. I gave them their toys and they ran away again. Down below they shouted at their mother and I could hear her struggling with the shopping. Then she appeared and leant in the doorway.

"Hello," she said. "How are you?"

"I'm tired," I said, "jet-lag. I'm going to have a rest as soon as I'm unpacked."

"What was it like?"

"Interesting really."

"I see you managed to bring your dirty washing back. Don't they have laundries in those five-star hotels?"

I didn't answer. I'd just got halfway down the suitcase and I could see the small clapper-board, yet I knew for certain that I'd left it on the Reverend's desk. I had watched one of his acolytes take it away with the ditty-bag. I picked it up and looked; the bottom had been screwed back into position. I shook it. Not a sound.

"Any messages?" I asked, just for something to say. "Any work?"

"I told you, those Mexicans came to see you. Said they'd been given your name by the girl at Matrix. They were producing some so-called big feature in Brazil. They said they were trying to put a very special film crew together. People had to get on well because it would be three months under difficult conditions. Difficult work too."

"So what happened? When is it for? Brazil."

"Don't pretend, Del. It didn't sound a bit like you . . . and that's what I told them. Three months in the jungle, a big feature. You've always said yourself . . ."

"Yes, I know. Still you should have phoned me."

"I wasn't going to make a phone call to California when

I knew you'd turn it down. It would have been a complete waste of money."

"Okay, any chance of a cup of coffee?"

She left the room and I took a screwdriver and undid the two screws. The wood came away and revealed a lot of cotton wool. I pulled it out and threw it into the bin under the dressing table. Then I tipped the board and twelve large diamonds rolled into my left hand. Twelve. By anybody's reckoning they must have been worth, I don't know, two hundred thousand pounds.

I moved to the window and looked down into the street. It was small, terribly small. An express went by and the cool rain began to spatter the grey tarmac of the road. So much money—that was the mortgage gone, and that was work gone too.

The Reverend had known me better than I'd known myself. Across a continent and across three thousand miles of ocean his hand had reached out and caught me by the heart. "What the Reverend says comes true; he has the power to make his dream actual." That's what Angela had said.

I squeezed the diamonds in my hand. I couldn't turn them down this time. I was free. There was a fortune in my hand and it could make me brave and daring. I could grow. I could do what I liked, in secret or out loud.

She came back into the room. "You're annoyed about that job, aren't you?" She put the mug of coffee onto the dressing table.

"No," I said. "Not now. I was offered something else, better. A bigger job, lots of money, out in Los Angeles, for keeps."

"I wouldn't want to live in America," she said. "All my

friends are here, and my father's all on his own now. The kids are doing well at school."

I felt the diamonds in my palm. So much light and freedom in one hand. I understood why people murdered for them. "It's a good job," I said. "I think you'd like it when you got there. Worth a try. The kids would love it. Big long beaches, summer all year long."

"Well, you can take it if you like. I wouldn't go."

There was silence and I slipped the diamonds into my pocket. I would have them valued tomorrow.

"Are you going to take it then?"

"It is an opportunity," I said, "too good to miss, really. I must say I'm tempted, sorely tempted. Nobody over here would offer me such a job." The words didn't sound like me but I said them just the same. I hesitated. "But I haven't made my mind up yet. I'll have to think about it." And I closed the suitcase and put it away on top of the wardrobe where I always put it.

MICHAEL DE LARRABEITI was born in London, England. He has worked as a documentary cameraman and as a travel guide in France, Spain, and Morocco. He's written eight other books, one of which, *The Borribles*—a children's adventure story about London runaways living in derelict houses and cellars—generated widespread controversy when it was published in England in 1976. Mr. de Larrabeiti now lives in an Oxfordshire village with his wife and three children. *The Hollywood Takes* is his second book for the Crime Club; his first, *The Bunce,* was a nominee for the British Crime Writers' Association's award for best novel of the year, and has been bought by the BBC for adaptation as a five-part serial.